Book One

Monster
Problems

By

R.L. Ullman

But That's
Another Story...
Press

Monster Problems

Cover design by Yusup Mediyan
All character images created with heromachine.com.

Published by But That's Another Story… Press
Ridgefield, CT

Printed in the United States of America.

First Printing, 2018.

ISBN: 978-0-9984129-2-4
Library of Congress Control Number: 2018905598

To Esther and Lillian,
thanks for looking out for me

PRAISE FOR MONSTER PROBLEMS
READERS' FAVORITE BOOK AWARD WINNER

"I absolutely loved Monster Problems. The story is action-packed and fast-paced. The characters were unique and lovable, as well as great role models. I was hooked by the first page and never wanted to put it down." **Rating: 5.0 stars by Kristen Van Kampen (Teen Reviewer).**

"Ullman spins a monstrosity of a tale in the first book of his new series. It reminds me of Harry Potter with a twist. Hilarious and so unexpected. This book is one to believe in." **Rating: 5.0 stars by Gail Kamer.**

"From the first sentence it draws you in and doesn't let go until you've come to the very end. Ullman hits all the bases with this one. I can't recommend this supernatural adventure highly enough!" **Rating: 5.0 stars by Sarah Westmoreland.**

"All the characters are portrayed so well they'll remain fresh in the minds of readers. Like me, readers will be keen to grab book 2 to see what happens next." **Rating: 5.0 stars by Mamta Madhaven.**

"Monster Problems is a grand romp that will thrill kids and forever-young adults alike. I'm thrilled it's just the first book in Ullman's new series. Most highly recommended." **Rating: 5.0 stars by Jack Magnus.**

TABLE OF CONTENTS

CHAPTER ONE

MY LIFE BITES

Clearly, I won't be getting any sleep.

Not after the thundering crash of my door against the wall. Or the snap of my window shade, which is now rapping annoyingly against the glass pane. Or the bright light shining in my eyes as daylight streams over my face.

Note to self: stop sleeping in rooms that don't lock from the inside.

"Well, well," comes a nasally voice. "This must be the special one himself."

Okay, here we go. I roll over reluctantly, squinting at the two goons hovering over me. Needless to say, their expressions are less than warm-and-fuzzy.

The first guy reminds me of a shark, with his pale, unblinking eyes and long, thin nose. He's short and wearing the most disturbing Christmas sweater I've ever seen, featuring a snowman swallowing a reindeer. For some reason, he's studying me like I'm some kind of a zoo animal while frantically scribbling notes on his clipboard.

The second guy could pass for Mr. Clean's stunt double, minus the earing and the charm. He's bald, dressed in all white like an orderly at a psychiatric hospital, and his biceps are twice the size of his head.

After our awkward three-way staredown, shark-face finally puts down his pen and says, "Mr. Abraham Matthews, I presume?"

"My friends call me Bram," I say. "So, you can call me Abraham."

Shark-face doesn't crack a smile. Instead, he looks down at his clipboard and presses on, "I see, Mr. Matthews, that you arrived in the wee hours of the morning. The night guard informed us you were hand-delivered by the police."

"Yep," I say. "They were in the neighborhood. Nice of the boys to give me a lift."

"I also understand," he says, "that you ran away from your group home three weeks ago—in Arizona."

"Ah, Arizona," I say. "Quite an interesting place. Did you know they'll arrest you for cutting down a cactus? Or that crazy roadrunner bird from the cartoon is actually real? Dynamite-carrying coyotes, however, not so much."

"You do realize, Mr. Matthews, that you are now in Massachusetts? That's over two-thousand five-hundred miles away."

"Really?" I say, faking a shiver. "No wonder I'm so darn cold."

"You're a funny guy," shark-face says. "But we can

be funny too. Isn't that right, Mr. Snide?"

"Hilarious," the bald guy says, cracking his knuckles.

"Do you know where you are?" shark-face asks.

"Well, I'm no detective," I say, taking a look around, "but I think you just told me I'm in Massachusetts." Other than these bozos and the giant daddy-long-legs hanging from the ceiling, the place has an all-too-familiar sparseness. There's a bed, a desk, and a closet, but that's about it.

"I'll be a little more specific," shark-face says. "You are at the New England Home for Troubled Boys. I am Mr. Glume, the Director, and my esteemed colleague here is Mr. Snide, the House Manager."

"Honored to make your acquaintance," I say. Truth be told, I've bounced around group homes like this my entire life. There was the one in Arizona. And before that California. And before that Oregon, and so on. I've been in so many of these joints I've lost count.

And they're all the same. They claim they'll find you a loving family. They claim you're just one step away from enjoying family movie nights and roasting marshmallows over a fire. But trust me, it never happens.

Not for kids like me.

Don't worry, there's no need to break out the violins. I'm a realist, so I know the odds are against me. After all, I'm twelve now, which means no first-time parents would touch me with a ten-foot pole. Think about it. Why would any wide-eyed, bushy-tailed couple looking to adopt take on a troubled teen when they could drive off the lot with a brand-new baby instead? Trust me, they wouldn't. As soon as you're out of diapers, you're considered damaged goods.

Plus, I've got my, well, other quirks…

As Glume flips through the mountain of paperwork on his clipboard, his whisper-thin eyebrows rise higher and higher. Clearly, he's got my whole case file.

"You've been in the foster system since you were an infant," Glume says.

"Yep," I say. "Guess that makes me the poster child."

"It says your parents died in a house fire," he continues. "What a shame."

"I've come to grips with it," I say quickly.

"I'm sure you have," Glume says. "But it also says you have quite a long history of causing trouble. Lots of trouble. In fact, the director of your former group home doesn't want you back. She says you have… unusual habits?"

"Like she should talk," I scoff. "She didn't get the nickname 'Beast of Bourbon' for nothing."

"She says you stay up all night. You refuse to go to bed during mandatory lights out."

"I'm a night owl," I say. "I catch my 'z's' during the daytime. Otherwise, I get cranky. Like now, for instance."

"She says you avoid sunlight."

"I burn easily," I say. "I'm delicate."

"And you only eat food that is red in color?"

"Okay, now even I have to admit that's a weird one. She's got me there."

Glume flips through more pages. "It seems several reports are accusing you of property damage—like flooding the basement."

"Not true," I say. "I walked in just as some kid threw the fire extinguisher into the washing machine. No one expected it to go off like that. The bubbles were insane."

"And the broken windows on the second floor?"

"Purely an accident," I counter. "They told us to do a craft project. Who knew taping worms to glass would attract so many birds?"

"And the bed bug infestation?"

"A complete misunderstanding," I say. "I was the one warning those kids to leave their pillows in the garbage dumpster."

"Mr. Matthews, you are not taking responsibility for your involvement in any of these incidents."

"That's right," I say. "Because I wasn't responsible."

"Clearly," Glume says. "In fact, you don't seem to be responsible for anything."

"Whew!" I say, wiping my brow. "I was worried we wouldn't understand each other."

"Well, you're in luck," Glume says. "I do understand you. I understand you perfectly. And fortunately for you, you've come to the right place."

"It sounds like it," I say relieved. Just then, my

stomach rumbles. I can't remember the last time I ate. "Hey, this has been a great kumbaya session, but how about we wrap it up and head to the kitchen for a hearty breakfast?"

"Excellent idea, Mr. Matthews," Glume says. "We shall adjourn to the kitchen where we will begin your education."

"Great, I could eat a—wait, did you say education?"

"Oh, don't panic, Mr. Matthews," Glume says with a sinister smile. "Here at the New England School for Troubled Boys, you'll get a steady diet of exactly what you need."

"And what's that?" I ask suspiciously.

"Responsibility," he says.

"Is this the hilarious part?" I ask.

"I guess that depends on which side of the clipboard you're standing on," Glume answers. "Now you can choose to get up on your own or, if you would like, Mr. Snide would be more than happy to assist you."

The bald guy steps forward and I realize this could get real ugly real fast. But I'm not looking for any trouble.

"Okay, hold your horses, cue ball," I say, throwing my legs over the side. "There's no need to get personal. Let's get this education thing over with so I can eat."

***

I don't think I've ever seen so many dishes in one

kitchen sink before. They're piled sky-high like Glume had been waiting for my arrival for weeks. And it isn't just plates. There are stacks of dirty cups, and hundreds of used forks and spoons scattered all over the place. At least they know enough to use plastic knives.

"Your first lesson begins now," Glume says gleefully. "Every one of these items needs to be hand-washed, hand-dried, and returned to its proper place."

"Hand washed?" I exclaim. "You mean, there's no dishwasher?"

"We just got a new one," Snide says, throwing a dish towel over my face. "Have fun."

"But... this will take hours," I say. "What about food?"

"Oh, you'll find plenty of leftovers," Glume says, "if you *lick* the plates clean. You'd best get started, Mr. Matthews. And please, no spots on the silverware."

As they exit, I hear them snickering down the hall. Well, this is a major bummer. I had hoped this would be a longer stop—get in a few square meals, sleep in a warm bed—but now I need to rethink my plans. After all, I didn't volunteer to be the resident Cinderella.

As I turn on the faucet, I catch my reflection in the stainless tea kettle. Not surprisingly, I look as tired as I feel. My skin is thin and pale, my dark hair is a tangled mess, and my eyes look like brown half-circles.

I take in the ceramic carnage around me and exhale.

I'm in no mood to do this chore the conventional

way, so I open the cabinets to see where everything is supposed to go, and peer over my shoulder to ensure the coast is clear.

Then, I get busy.

Remember those quirks I mentioned earlier? Well, sometimes they come in handy. Like right now.

You see, I have some strange abilities.

Super speed happens to be one of them.

Now I'm not claiming to be the Flash or anything, but I can really motor when I need to. I've never told anyone about it. I mean, people think I'm weird enough already. But when a situation calls for it and no one's around, I like to indulge a little.

The only problem is that using my super speed wipes me out. Especially if I haven't eaten in a while. But this task is simply too inhumane not to go for it.

So, despite some ear-jarring dish clinking, I manage to wash, dry, and put away every item in less than two minutes with no spots on the silverware. I stand back and admire my handiwork.

Even though I'm feeling drained, it was worth it. And the best part is that no one will be the wiser.

At least, that's what I think.

Until I turn around.

That's when I find a blond, curly-haired kid standing behind me with his jaw hanging open. He looks a few years younger than me, and he's holding a dirty plate.

I curse under my breath for being so careless.

Time to play it cool.

"Thanks," I say, taking the plate out of his hands as if nothing happened. "I must have missed that one."

I turn back to the sink and begin washing it—at normal speed. Okay, don't panic. Maybe he didn't see anything.

"D-Do you have superpowers?" he stammers.

Or maybe not.

"What are you talking about?" I say, grabbing the dish towel to start drying.

"Y-You just cleaned that mess up ridiculously fast," he says. "I-I saw you do it."

"Really?" I say, putting the plate away. I hate lying to the kid, but what choice do I have? "So, let me ask you something. If I could move like that, do you think I'd be hanging around this joy factory? Believe me, I'd take off so fast all you'd see is a cloud of dust."

"Well," the boy says, thinking it over, "I-I guess that's true."

"Believe me, I wish I had superpowers like that. Yet, here we are. Hey, are you feeling okay? You look kind of green. Maybe you need to sit down?"

The boy looks confused. "I... but... I... Maybe I'm not feeling so well."

"Here," I say, pulling over a chair from the table in the corner. "Take a load off."

As he slumps down, I fill a glass with water and get him some ice. "Drink this. Maybe you're dehydrated.

Kids today don't drink enough water."

"Thanks," he says, downing half the glass in one gulp. "Sorry, I… must be losing my mind."

"No problem," I say, taking a seat beside him and reaching out my hand. "My name is Abraham. But you can call me Bram."

"I'm Johnny," he says, shaking my hand. "You're that kid who came in late last night. With the police."

"The one and only," I say. "Sorry if I woke you."

"No big deal," he says. "I sleep with one eye open anyway. Have for a while."

"Yeah," I say. "I get it."

"So, how'd you end up here?" he asks, taking another sip.

"Incredible luck?" I say, causing Johnny to spit take.

"Seriously," I continue. "I don't know. I've been in foster care as long as I can remember. I've probably lived with twenty foster families. Eventually, no one wanted me anymore, so now I just kind of go from group home to group home."

"Twenty families?" he says, either shocked or impressed. "That's a lot of foster families."

"I guess," I say with a shrug. "I never really thought about it. I mean, it's all kind of a blur now. I just remember it was hard to keep track of all the different rules. What was okay in one house would be against the law in the next. I guess I never felt settled, you know? How about you? How'd you get here?"

"I got labeled a 'bad kid' a few years back,'" he says, sitting back. "I had just gotten to a new family. Nice couple who already had a biological son. At first, I thought I had a chance. Well, I guess the kid wasn't so happy I was there and claimed I stole his mom's necklace. It was ridiculous. I've never stolen anything in my life! Anyway, he wasn't going anywhere so I got the boot. Been here ever since."

"That's rough," I say. "I can't even tell you how many times I've been blamed for stuff I didn't do. I actually had one parent tell me if her daughter and I were hanging off a cliff and she could only save one of us, she'd save her kid every single time. Like, isn't that obvious? But I always wondered why she had to say it. It's just cruel, you know?"

"I guess kids like us don't get to have real families," Johnny says, his face falling.

For some reason, his words hit me hard.

"Yeah," I say. "I guess so."

We sit in silence for a minute when I notice a newspaper on the table. The headline reads:

GRAVE ROBBERS EXHUME BODY OF MILITARY HERO

"Well, that's creepy," I say.

"Yeah," Johnny says. "It was all over the news. It was the grave of some old military sharpshooter who helped win a bunch of wars. Someone dug him up and took all his bones. I think it's the second grave robbery in the last two weeks. People are weird."

"Totally weird," I agree, wondering why anyone would even think about doing something like that.

"Well, it's not so bad here," Johnny says, trying to change the subject. "As long as you follow the rules."

"Guess I'm in trouble then," I say. "Because I'm not much of a rule-follower."

"I wasn't either," he says. "Until I got here."

Just then, the door bursts open, and Snide barges in. "How're the chores go—What?"

The ogre stops short, taking in the scene.

"Oh, I'm all finished," I say quickly. "Guess I'm more of a Type A personality than I thought. I was just using my free time here to meet some of my fellow inmates."

"But that's impossible!" Snide says furiously. "You couldn't have done it all alone." Then, he wheels on Johnny. "You helped him!"

"No," I interject. "He didn't lift a finger."

"I think I'll be going now," Johnny says, standing up quickly. He shoots me a look, mouths 'good luck,' and makes a brisk exit.

"I don't believe you," the brute says.

"It's all in the magic of the suds," I claim, holding out my arms. "And look, no dish-pan hands."

"That's it, wise guy!" he says. "You're coming with

me!"

"To where?" I ask, as Snide opens the kitchen door and waves me into the hallway.

"You'll see," Snide says, as we walk down the hall and past an office where Glume is on the phone.

"Oh, yes, Officer Smith," Glume says into the receiver. Then he catches sight of us and breaks into a weird smile. "Mr. Matthews is having a great time. He's learning the ropes quickly."

Snide chuckles and leads me down a flight of stairs.

"Hope you're not afraid of the dark," he says.

Well, he's right about one thing, wherever he's taking me is dark—pitch dark even. But not for me. For some reason, I've always been able to see perfectly in darkness. It's like my eyes never need time to adjust. Of course, I have no idea why. I guess it's just another one of my strange quirks.

But when we reach the bottom, Snide flicks on a dim light, and my stomach drops. The basement is totally creepy, with cement-block walls and a way-too-low ceiling. It smells musty down here, like mold has been brewing for centuries.

Then, I notice a row of steel doors lining the walls.

What are those for?

Snide reaches into his back pocket and pulls out a set of keys. As he jingles them around the ring, they echo through the narrow chamber. Finally, he finds the one he's looking for.

"Um, is this some kind of a kid dungeon?" I ask. "Because I don't think state-sponsored group homes are supposed to have kid dungeons."

"You think you've got it all figured out, don't you Matthews?" he says, unlocking the steel door to our left. "Well, keep thinking that way and you're gonna have problems around here. Serious problems."

"C'mon," I plead, "you're not really gonna—"

But before I can finish my sentence, he nudges me inside the tiny cell. And then he slams the door shut behind me.

Suddenly, a small slat opens at the top of the door, and Snide presses his ugly mug into the opening.

"Do you know what we do with problems here at the New England Home for Troubled Boys?"

I'm about to provide an eloquent response when I realize the question is rhetorical.

"We keep 'em down here in solitary," he says. "Until one way or another, they aren't problems anymore."

Then, he slams the slat closed.

And I'm locked inside.

Foster Care Profile

Case No: 66649666

Name: <u>MATTHEWS, ABRAHAM</u>
Nickname(s): <u>BRAM</u>
Yrs in Care: <u>12 years</u>
Difficulty: <u>HIGH</u>

VITALS:
Height: <u>4'10"</u>
Weight: <u>95lbs</u>
Hair: <u>Black</u>
Eyes: <u>Brown</u>

FOSTER CARE R
ARIZONA, PHOE
CALIFORNIA,
OREGON, SALE
IDAHO, BOISE
NEVADA, RENO
CALIFORNIA,
UTAH, LOGAN
WYOMING, CA
NEW MEXICO, ALBEQUERQUE
PENNSYLVANIA, ERIE (ran away after 3 mo.)
(Please see pages 2-4 for additional foster locations)

Matthews, Abraham (Bram)   pg 1/56

CHAPTER TWO

BREAKING AND EXITING

You'd be surprised how time doesn't fly when you're locked inside a basement prison cell.

Let's just say there's way too much time to think. In fact, I've spent so much time thinking, the mere thought of thinking absolutely exhausts me. Especially after holding a spirited debate with myself about whether I'm hungrier or thirstier. Now I fear I'm drifting into a dangerous state of delusion.

Case in point, there seems to be a hunk of crusty bread lying by the foot of the door. I haven't got the foggiest idea how it got there. I mean, I certainly would have noticed if someone had opened the door or dropped it through the slat.

Or would I?

I stare at the bread for a good long while, questioning if it's even real until I muster enough energy to poke it with my foot. The bread tumbles across the floor, hits the wall, and comes to a dead stop.

Okay, at least I'm not seeing things.

Unfortunately, the sight of the bread utterly repulses me. Look, I don't know why I can only eat red-colored food. Again, I had hours to contemplate that one too. My conclusion—I'm a freak. So, I'm clearly going to starve to death unless I can get out of here.

Looking up, I notice a small spider weaving an intricate web in the corner of the ceiling. For some reason, wherever I go spiders seem to follow.

Maybe they're my spirit insect.

I wonder why this one is so darn industrious. After all, there aren't any flies buzzing around. And every time I check in on the little guy, its web is not only getting larger, but closer. So, either we'll die in here together, or it's plotting to take early retirement from its largest catch ever—me!

So yeah, I'm a little delusional. But what happens next pushes me over the edge.

First, I hear little pitter-patter noises. Like something is scampering across the cement floor. I sit up and look around, but I don't see anything.

Then, they come into view.

Two hairy rats are inspecting the bread. One is tall and thin, the other small and fat. They sniff it with their pink noses, sinking their claws into the hard crust. They squeak back and forth, chattering away when suddenly their squeaks turn into... words?

"See here food me told you me smelt," the fat one says.

"Right you be," the thin one says, looking at me. "Pink one eat not."

I clean out my ears with my fingers. Are they actually speaking English or am I actually nuts?

"Lose out does he," the fat one says, taking a big bite. "Stupid maybe he be."

"Blind maybe he be," the thin one says, taking a bite of his own.

"Stupid and blind maybe he be," the fat one says, and they both cackle at my expense.

Okay, that's enough. After the day I've had I'm not about to sit here and get insulted by vermin.

So, I lean over and interject, "Pink one bread no like maybe?"

They freeze.

A piece of bread drops from the thin one's mouth.

Then, they look at each other, and then back at me.

"P-Pink one talk us like?" the thin one stammers.

The fat one swallows hard and slowly backs up. "P-Pink one … me understands?"

"Look, you can have the bread," I say. "Seriously, I'm not going to eat it."

"Impossible this be!" the thin one says.

"Unless … unless …" the fat one says, staring at me. Then, he takes off like his ears are on fire, disappearing through a narrow crevice between the cement blocks.

"Hey, wait!" I call out. "Unless what?" I look at the thin one. "What's he talking about?"

The rat looks at me, then at the bread, then back at me. Then he grabs a chunk of crust and hightails it after his friend.

At this point, I realize my mind is playing tricks on me and I can't distinguish between fantasy and reality. I mean, I'm so far gone I'm speaking Rat!

Suddenly, the room starts spinning. I'm guessing starvation has finally caught up with me. My body starts trembling and I can't seem to keep my eyes open.

I'm losing consciousness.

Fading out.

I look up to say goodbye to my spider friend, but to my surprise, its web is still there, but the spider is gone.

Then, everything goes black.

***

It takes all I have just to open my eyes, but the bright light overhead forces them closed again. My head is throbbing, and I feel like I've been run over by a steamroller. It's not until I try sitting up that I realize I'm not lying on a cement floor anymore, but on a bed. I'm tucked under the covers and my head is resting on a soft pillow. I try propping up again, but I don't get far.

"Take it easy," comes a familiar voice.

I pry my eyes open to find Johnny sitting beside me. He's holding out a plate with something red on it.

Swedish Fish candies!

"H-How did you know?" I ask.

"You kept moaning for something red to eat," Johnny says. "I didn't have much time, so I snuck down to the kitchen and grabbed these. Although technically I'm not sure Swedish Fish actually qualify as food."

"It's perfect," I say, inhaling the delicious treats. After being so hungry for so long, I can feel the sugar entering my bloodstream, re-energizing my body. "Where am I? What are you doing here?"

"After you passed out, they pulled you out of the dungeon and brought you back to your room. I felt bad seeing what they did to you. So, after everyone went to bed, I snuck in to check on you. But I can't stay long. Snide's on night duty."

Out of the corner of my eye, I catch a digital clock sitting on a desk. It reads: 12:49 am. It's the middle of the night. "How long was I down there?"

"Sixteen hours," Johnny says. "I think that's a record. By the way, why do you only eat red stuff?"

"Because I'm weird," I say, swallowing the last Swedish Fish. "Thanks for getting this for me. I was starving."

"Clearly," Johnny says. "They put all the new kids in the dungeon. Although they usually spring them after four hours. So, you must have made one heck of a first impression."

"Well, my first impression will be my last," I say. "Because I'm getting out of here. ASAP."

"What?" Johnny says. "Are you nuts? Where are you going to go?"

"Doesn't matter," I say, peeling back the covers and getting to my feet. I stand up, although I feel pretty shaky. "But wherever I'll be, it won't be here."

"But how will you survive?" Johnny asks. "If you're here, at least you've got food and shelter."

"Let's get something straight," I say, looking him straight in the eyes. "Some things are more important than food and shelter. Just because they put every kid in a dungeon doesn't make it okay. We're human beings, not monsters."

Johnny's lips quiver as he tries to respond, but he can't. I didn't mean to upset him, but what's happening here isn't right. It's like the old story of the frog and the pot of boiling water. If you put the frog straight into a pot of boiling water, it'll feel the heat and jump right out. But if the frog is put into warm water and you turn up the heat slowly, the frog won't notice the temperature rising and will end up being boiled alive.

Johnny's been here so long everything seems normal to him, but I'm not going to wait around until I get cooked. I look out the window. We're on the third floor, which is way too high to jump. If I'm going to make my exit, I'll have to do it through the front door.

Which means I'll need to dodge Snide.

"Thanks for your help," I say, grabbing my gray hoodie from the back of the door. "Do you want to come with me?"

At first, Johnny looks stunned by my question. Then, he sits quietly for a moment, deep in thought.

"No, but thanks," he says finally. "I kind of watch over some of the smaller guys here. I guess this is my home now."

His answer doesn't surprise me. Kids like us tend to accept our situations, no matter how bad they may be. But over time I've learned to follow my instincts on what I think is right, not comfortable. Still, I can't just leave him and the other kids in this horrible mess.

Then, I get an idea.

"Don't worry," I say. "I'll help you out before I go."

"Thanks," he says. "So, is this the part where I see a cloud of dust?"

I smile. Clearly, I never had him fooled.

"Something like that," I say. "Take care of yourself."

He nods, and I enter the hall.

It's pitch black, but again, darkness isn't a problem for me. Johnny was right though. I could turn on my super speed and make a clean getaway, but I plan on saving it for later. After all, that's how I ended up here in the first place. I got too tired to outrun the police.

Since everyone is asleep, I tiptoe down the stairs, passing Glume's room on the second floor. The door is cracked and old shark-face is peacefully snoring away. Sleep while you can because your whole world is about to change.

When I reach the bottom step, I have a clear pathway to the front door. My instincts tell me to go for it, but I can't. I promised Johnny I'd help him out.

So, I turn the corner and head for the office. The door is open, and the lights are on, but no one is inside. Snide must be doing his rounds.

I enter the room and duck behind the desk. Then, I pop up to dial the phone and pull the receiver back down with me. The phone rings once before someone picks up.

"This is 9-1-1, how can we assist you?" the female operator says.

"Yes, hi, I'm calling from the New England Home for Troubled Boys. I'd like to report on the improper treatment of children here."

"Are you a child?" the operator asks, her voice sounding surprised.

"Yes," I say. "I'm a resident here."

"Oh," she says. "What kind of improper treatment?"

I don't have much time, so I cut to the chase. "Just get the police here. Tell them to go straight to the basement. There's a kid dungeon down there no one knows about. You'll see. Just hurry."

"I've already sent a notification to the police," the operator says. "They should be there shortly. Are you okay? Can I have your name?"

I think about giving my name, but instead, I say, "Look, I represent all the kids here. Good kids that just need a helping hand."

Then, I hang up. I need to split before Snide shows up. But when I leap back into the hallway, I discover a large figure blocking my path to the front door.

Snide!

"What were you doing in my office, Matthews?"

"I'm a night owl, remember?"

The oaf smiles. "Are you looking for your file, Matthews? Are you trying to find out why no one loves you?"

"Shut up, Snide," I say.

"That's Mr. Snide," he says.

"Shut up, Mr. Snide," I say.

"Well, I'll tell you something you probably didn't know," Snide says. "Because I did a little research on you myself."

"Congratulations," I say. "Because I didn't think Neanderthals could read."

"Ha," Snide says. "Then I guess you're not interested in what I found out. It's about your daddy."

He stands there with a big, stupid grin on his face. He's baiting me. Sucking me in. But what could he have found out about my dad? I mean, he's long dead.

"Okay," I say, my curiosity getting the best of me. "I'll bite, what is it?"

"Get this," Snide says, folding his immense arms. "You weren't put into foster care by just anyone. Your very own father dropped you into the system."

What?

I'm stunned. That's not what I'd been told. I was told my parents died in a fire that I somehow survived, and then I was put into foster care. So, what he's saying can't be true.

"You're lying," I say.

"Am I, Matthews?" he says. "Well, I did some digging. Your case is so darn thick and convoluted it took a while. But I went all the way back and found your very first record and guess what? Your daddy's signature was right on it. Mr. Gabriel Matthews. He gave you away like a smelly carpet."

No way. That's impossible.

"Must be tough," Snide continues, "but I guess you can say you've been unwanted your whole life."

"Liar!" I yell, red hot. All I want to do is get out of here, but Snide is blocking the hallway.

"Now go back to your room, Matthews," he orders.

"No," I answer.

"I was hoping you'd say that," he says.

Then, he cracks his knuckles, and charges at me!

Without thinking, I react.

Just before Snide reaches me, I turn on my super speed and somersault between his legs in a flash. Snide thunders over me and crashes into a table which breaks beneath his considerable weight.

"I don't know how you did that," he says, standing up, his muscles rippling. "But you're going to pay."

If he catches me, he'll tear me limb from limb.

Suddenly, the hall light clicks on.

"Snide?"

That's Glume's voice!

"Snide, what's all the ruckus?"

As Snide looks up, I realize this may be my only chance. The Swedish Fish aren't going to last in my system for long, so my speed powers will be nearing the end of their shelf life. If I'm getting out it has to be now!

I bolt down the hall and plow into the front door, knocking it clear off its hinges. Oh well, I guess Glume can add that to my list of property damage. My shoulder is throbbing but I don't stop. I book down the street as fast as I can, my speed waning with every step. When I think I'm a good enough distance away, I duck behind a parked pickup truck.

Just then, I hear SIRENS—police sirens!

Four patrol cars pull up in front of the group home. I peer around the truck as a bunch of police officers sprint up the front steps, disappearing through the open door frame I left behind. I watch anxiously from my hiding spot, hoping the boys in blue got my instructions.

After what seems like an eternity, there's movement.

First, I see Glume, and then Snide. They're being led out of the building—in handcuffs!

It worked!

Suddenly, boys spill out of the house onto the front steps. They all look shell-shocked as they watch Glume and Snide get pushed into the back of a police car. But there's one boy in the middle of the pack who is wearing a different expression.

He has blond, curly hair. And he's smiling.

***

As I roam the city in the dead of night, I'm feeling pretty lost. After all of this, there's no way I can ever go to another group home again. Plus, I'm pretty sure if the police catch me, I'll be charged with reverse breaking and entering.

So, for the first time, I'm truly on my own.

And what's worse, I can't stop thinking about what Snide said. Was everything I thought I knew about my life a lie? Did my father really put me into foster care? Did my parents really not want me?

Suddenly, a HOWL in the distance snaps me back to reality. It sounds like a wounded dog. Looking around, I realize I wandered into a graveyard of all places.

Lucky me.

I keep walking, reading the tombstones around me. Some are really old, like as far back as the 1800s. Then, I remember that eerie story about the graverobbers and a chill runs down my spine.

I can keep going, but I'm pretty hungry. If I don't eat something soon, I'll pass out. But the graveyard just seems to go on and on, and my chances of finding a pizza joint in a place like this are slim to none.

I turn to head back when another HOWL pierces the night air, making the hairs on the back of my neck stand on end. That one seemed a lot closer than the last one.

Looking up, I realize there's a full moon.

Wonderful.

I pull my hood over my head and start walking double time. To my relief, I finally find the exit and step through the gates, only to hear RUSTLING behind me.

I spin around and gasp.

Because standing in front of me is a hunched figure.

At first, I think it's a man, but there's something wrong with his head. Then, he steps onto the pavement and I realize it isn't a man at all. His head is shaped like a wolf, and every inch of his muscular body is covered in matted, brown fur.

My jaw hits the floor.

Holy cow!

I can't believe what I'm seeing.

It's a... a... werewolf?!?

The beast stares at me with his bright red eyes as a long string of drool drips from the corner of his mouth, splattering onto the pavement.

I want to move, but I'm glued to the spot.

Then, he lets out an ear-piercing HOWL.

And to my horror, several creatures HOWL back.

MONSTEROLOGY 101 FIELD GUIDE

WEREWOLF

CLASSIFICATION:

Type: Shapeshifter
Sub-Type: Lycanthrope
Height: Variable
Weight: Variable
Eye Color: Red
Hair Color: Variable

KNOWN ABILITIES:

- Transformations typically occur during a full moon
- Superhuman Strength, Speed, Reflexes, Agility, and Healing
- Heightened Sight, Smell and Hearing

KNOWN WEAKNESSES:

- Vulnerable to silver objects (e.g. bullets or blades)
- Susceptible to injury in human form
- Wolfsbane is rumored to reverse lycanthropy

DANGER LEVEL:

HIGH

TIPS TO AVOID AN UNWANTED ENCOUNTER:

- Remain inside during a full moon
- Mask your scent
- Travel in large crowds
- Stay far away from wooded areas

CHAPTER THREE

HERE A WEREWOLF, THERE A WEREWOLF

Despite my limited knowledge of low budget B-movies, I'm pretty sure the creature staring me down meets all the criteria for a bonafide werewolf.

Angry wolf face. Check.

Smelly, furry body. Double check.

Clear intention to kill me. Triple check.

That's when my fight or flight mode kicks in. There's no question I'm choosing flight, but I'd already used up my super speed escaping from Snide. I've got nothing left in the tank!

Based on the look in the beast's eyes, I have no doubt he'll tear me to shreds as soon as I move a muscle. Then again, if I just stand here doing nothing, I'm pretty sure he'll tear me to shreds anyway. So, I guess this is a lose-lose situation.

Maybe Johnny was right. Maybe I should've just stayed at the New England Home for Troubled Boys. After all, what's a little torture compared with losing your life forever?

Then, I realize something.

The werewolf hasn't attacked me.

Why hasn't he attacked me?

I mean, he's got me cornered. He easily could have gobbled me up by now and had cheesecake for dessert. Yet, he hasn't moved. Why not?

At this point, I've got nothing to lose, so I figure I'll test the waters.

"Um, if you don't mind," I say, "I've got to go. You see I've got this huge book report on some dead guy due tomorrow, and I haven't even started the darn book yet. You look like you've been in that situation a few times yourself. So, anyway, I hope you have a great night."

I take a step backward and the werewolf lets out a deep-throated growl. Then, he steps towards me.

Okay, he didn't like that. But then again, he still hasn't pounced on me either.

That's when I get a crazy thought.

I take a step to my left.

The werewolf steps right, staying in front of me.

Weird.

I step right. He steps left.

Still in front of me.

Great. I'm square dancing with a werewolf.

For some reason, wherever I go he wants to keep me dead in his sights. But there's one direction I haven't tried yet. Of course, this could mean certain death.

Here goes nothing.

I say a prayer and take a step forward.

The werewolf's eyes grow big, and he leaps ten feet backward, snarling. Well, I wasn't expecting that! It almost seems like he's afraid of me.

How's that even possible?

But I'll have to figure that out later because this might be my only chance to escape. I wheel around to bolt when, to my surprise, two other creatures leap out of the woods, scaring the bejesus out of me.

More werewolves!

These two are just as big as the first one, except one is black and the other is light brown. And now, with his buddies present, werewolf number one seems to have regained his confidence, because he lets out a series of sharp hoots, like he's barking orders.

Suddenly, the three spread out around me.

I'm surrounded!

If I don't come up with a plan, I'll be mincemeat. Maybe I can get the first one to back up again so I can make a break for it? I step towards him, but this time he doesn't budge. Instead, he roars back with such foul-smelling ferocity it makes me wish I was wearing a gas mask.

Well, that didn't work.

In fact, I think I made him angrier.

Suddenly, panic sets in. How could I be so stupid to think a kid-eating werewolf was scared of me? He was probably just keeping an eye on me until his friends showed up. After all, who likes dining alone?

Then, they move in.

I start hyperventilating.

Everywhere I look, all I see are teeth, fur, and claws. Is this how it's going to end? I can see the headlines now: *Loner Kid Mauled by Angry Gang of Werewolves.*

I close my eyes and brace myself for the first slash of claws. But instead, I feel something... different.

Something light lands over my head and body.

I open my eyes to find I'm covered in a thin, white netting. It's sticky and sort of tickles where it touches my skin. What's going on?

The next thing I know, the net tightens, cinching my arms against my sides. I try extending my elbows, but I can't. It's too strong.

Suddenly, I'm lifted clear into the air and over the surprised faces of my wolfish friends. I'm flying high above the trees, far away from danger.

Yes! I'm saved!

But then I realize I'm not getting any higher. I hang in the air for a moment and my stomach lurches.

And then gravity does its thing.

No! I'm going to go splat!

My stomach drops, and I start plummeting towards the ground at ridiculous speed, my arms still pinned to my sides. So, I do what any reasonable person would do in a situation like this—I scream my lungs out!

The ground is approaching fast, and depending on which end I land on, I'll either break my head or my legs. I close my eyes, seconds away from impact. But instead of bouncing off the ground, someone catches me in the nick of time.

In fact, it seems like a whole group of people catch me all at once because I feel multiple arms cushioning different parts of my body. I'm so relieved I decide right then and there to dedicate the rest of my life to every person who saved me.

But it's not until I open my eyes that I realize I'll have more free time on my hands than I thought, because I'm not lying in the arms of multiple people, but rather one person with multiple arms!

I do a double take.

Okay, I'm clearly being held by a man. I mean, he looks like a normal man, with dark hair, a bushy beard, and a warm smile. But then I realize he's holding me in all of his arms, two of which are completely normal, but the other four looks like the appendages of… a spider?

I nearly pass out.

"Don't worry," he says. "I've got you."

"A-Are you Spiderman's brother?" I stammer.

"Something like that," he says with a wink.

He swipes down with one of his spider legs and cuts the strange wrapping from my body. Finally, my arms are free! I touch the material. It's a spider web! The thickest spider web I've ever seen.

It's only when he sets me on my feet that I realize how massive he is. He's tall and super muscular. But of course, his size isn't his most notable feature. That distinction belongs to his limbs. There are eight in total: two normal arms, two normal legs, and four spider legs—two on each side of his torso.

I close my eyes. Maybe this is all just a weird dream. But when I open them again, he's still standing there—spider legs and all.

"You okay?" he asks.

"Me? Oh, I'm great," I say. "Just another day talking casually with an enormous man-spider."

"Did the werewolves bite you?" he asks.

"No," I say. "They didn't touch me."

"You're lucky. If a werewolf bites you, you'll likely turn into one yourself."

"Well, isn't that a kick in the pants," I say.

"Listen, we've got to get out of here," he says.

I agree with that. But to where? And I don't even know this guy's name. If I can just get some food in me, I can use my speed and make my getaway.

"Yeah," I say. "About that. Look, I really appreciate you saving me and all, but I think I'm just gonna go solo from here on out. You wouldn't happen to have a tomato or a red pepper on you?"

The giant looks down at me and shakes his head.

"Kid, do you really think you're going to just walk out of here like nothing happened? Do you even know why those hounds are after you?"

Well, now I feel totally stupid.

"Of course I know," I say, faking it. "It's because, um … one time I … okay, I've got nothing."

"Let me simplify it," he says. "They're after one thing and they won't stop until they get it. And that's you."

"Me? Why would those shag carpets be after me? What did I do to them?"

"You were born," he says. "And now you've been discovered."

"Um, could you possibly be any more cryptic?"

"Okay, listen up because I'm gonna have to make this quick," he says, his eyes darting all around. "You see, we've been watching you. We knew this would happen one day. We just didn't think it would be today."

"Wait," I say. "What do you mean you've been watching me?"

He puffs up his chest and says, "Let's just say I have an extensive net-work." Then, he wiggles his spider legs.

"Net-work? What are you—"

Then, it hits me.

I suddenly realize what he's talking about. He's part spider. There was a spider in my room when I got to the New England Home for Troubled Boys. There was a spider in the dungeon. Then my mind flashes back to all of the spiders I've seen throughout my life and I realize they've always been there. Every foster family. Every group home. Everywhere.

Holy tarantulas!

Those spiders weren't random. They were a network of spies! My entire life has been bugged!

I back away, my heart racing. "Who are you? What do you want from me?"

"I go by Crawler," he says. "For obvious reasons. I know I look strange and what I'm telling you may sound crazy, but I'm what's called a 'Supernatural.' And so are you."

"A 'Super-what?'" I ask, totally lost. "What are you talking about?"

"You're a Supernatural, Bram," Crawler repeats.

"How do you know my na—?" I start, but then I remember. "Right, your spider spy network thingy."

"Here's how it breaks down," he says. "In this world, you're either a 'Natural,' which is a person without special abilities, or a 'Supernatural,' otherwise known as a person with special abilities. Guess which you are?"

"Normal?" I say.

"Really?" Crawler says. "My mistake. I thought you were the kid with super speed and a bad habit of getting burned in sunlight."

Well, I guess he knows me alright.

"Okay," I say. "So, let's just say I'm one of those things you mentioned. I still don't get why this is all happening now."

Crawler smiles. "Let's just say that 'now' we're not the only ones who know about you. You're a special kind of Supernatural."

"Special?" I say with a laugh. Now I'm convinced this is a case of mistaken identity. "And by the way, who is this 'we' you keep talking about?"

But before he can answer, there's a SNAP!

The werewolves have found us!

"We've wasted too much time," Crawler says, stepping in front of me. "Stay back."

I see the two brown werewolves, but where's the—

"Duck!" Crawler yells.

I hit the deck just as Crawler swings two of his spider legs over my head, firing off a series of webs. When I look up the black werewolf is pinned to a tree, only a few feet behind me. The creature struggles to get free, but the webbing is too strong.

Then, Crawler spins and lets loose an onslaught of spiderwebs. But the other two are too fast, disappearing into the brush.

"We've got to get out of here," Crawler says. "They'll be back soon. They're probably marshaling reinforcements."

"Wait, you mean there's more of them?"

"A lot more," he says. "It's time to go. Come on."

Then, he reaches out his hand.

But for some reason, I hesitate.

"Aren't you coming?" he asks.

I don't know why I paused. Maybe it's because I'm nuts. Or maybe it's because I don't know who he's working for. But deep down, I sense that if I go with him, everything in my life will change—and it may not be for the better.

Suddenly, HOWLS fill the air.

"Let's get out of here," I say, grabbing his hand.

Crawler scoops me onto his back and sprints. With his long stride and extra limbs, the guy can really move. I hold on for dear life, dodging branches as we weave through the trees. A few minutes later, we come upon a clearing where a motorcycle is parked. It's a chopper, with a long front-end and extended handlebar. For a second, I wonder if I'll be riding piggyback, but as we get closer I see a sidecar.

Crawler climbs on and lowers me into the seat. Then, he buckles my seatbelt with his spider legs and pops a helmet onto my head.

There are a series of HOWLS behind us. I turn to see a swarm of dots in the distance: four, then ten, then twenty.

The werewolves are heading straight for us!

"Gun it!" I yell.

"Hang on," Crawler says coolly. Then he puts on a pair of sunglasses, kickstarts the engine, and we're off.

CLASSIFIED

Person(s) of Interest

CODE NAME: CRAWLER

REAL NAME: UNKNOWN

BASE OF OPERATIONS: VAN HELSING ACADEMY

FACTS: Crawler operates as a field agent for Headmaster Lothar Van Helsing. Crawler's skills are primarily utilized for a variety of sensitive assignments including rescue and stealth missions. Crawler is armed and dangerous and should be approached with caution.

FIELD OBSERVATIONS:

- Possesses four spider appendages with super-human strength
- Can shoot webs and climb walls
- Communicates with all types of spiders

Category: Abnormal

Sub-Type: Not Applicable

Height: 6'5"

Weight: 240 lbs

STATUS: ACTIVE TARGET

DEPARTMENT OF SUPERNATURAL INVESTIGATIONS

[40]

CHAPTER FOUR

WELCOME TO WEIRDVILLE

I wake with a start.

Unfortunately, I'm not lying in bed at the New England Home for Troubled Boys just having a bad dream. Instead, I'm riding shotgun with a man-spider on a motorcycle. My head is throbbing, and my tongue feels like I've been chewing on a sock. I must have passed out, which isn't surprising given all of the energy I expended during the whole werewolf incident.

Speaking of werewolves.

I take in our surroundings and realize we're driving down some deserted road without a werewolf in sight. I don't know how long I've been out, but it must have been a while because the sun is now peeking over the horizon. I have to give major props to Crawler for getting us to safety relatively unscathed, my long-term therapy bills notwithstanding.

I slump back into the sidecar. So much has happened it's hard to process it all. According to Crawler, I'm some kind of a 'Supernatural,' whatever that means. And because of that, I'm now kidnapping target numero uno for a band of rabid werewolves.

That alone is crazy, but toss in Snide's comments about my dad being the one who dropped me into foster care and I'm still reeling. I mean, was Snide telling me the truth, or was he just pushing my buttons?

I need answers, and I'm about to ask Crawler some very pointed questions when he suddenly announces—

"We're here."

I look up just in time to see a black sign on the side of the road. At first, it's blank, but then bold, white letters appear out of nowhere. That's weird. My eyes must be playing tricks on me. Anyway, the sign reads:

VAN HELSING ACADEMY

Van Helsing what?!?

"Wait a minute," I yell over the engine. "Are you taking me to a school?"

"Something like that," Crawler yells back.

My back tenses up. School is not—and never will be—my thing. I'm not a good student, which is probably because I never spent any meaningful time at one school. Moving from family to family meant moving from school to school. And when you spend your life being fumbled around like a football, you tend not to make friends or get attention from teachers who think you're just passing through.

So, if this is where he's taking me, I won't be sticking around for long.

Suddenly, Crawler goes off-roading through the woods, bouncing me along some bumpy path I didn't see before. And the next thing I know, we're riding beside a huge brick wall. It's thirty feet tall and several miles long, with barbed wire wrapped around the top. Okay, I don't know any schools that need this kind of security. I mean, if I didn't catch the sign on the way in, I'd think we were visiting a prison.

Crawler rolls up to the main entrance. The massive front gate is closed shut, and the security booth is unmanned. Then, I notice a giant, yellow sign plastered front-and-center on the gate door. It reads:

RESTRICTED AREA.
DO NOT ENTER.
AUTHORIZED PERSONNEL ONLY.

Well, that's unwelcoming.

Needless to say, this doesn't look good.

"We're not seriously going in there, are we?" I ask.

"Yep," Crawler says. "We seriously are."

The next thing I know, a small device extends from the side of the security booth. At first, I think it's a microphone, but then it emits a thin, red light—like a laser. Crawler puts his face in front of it and it scans his pupils. Seconds later, the gate slides open with a slow and eerie screech.

Before I can object, Crawler powers us forward and I watch the gate close quickly behind us. Great. I guess there's no turning back now. But when I face forward, my jaw drops, because what's on the inside looks nothing like what's on the outside.

In fact, it looks like we're riding onto the movie set of an amazing prep school campus, with rolling green hills, expertly trimmed hedges, and stately brick buildings. Now I'm totally confused. Why would a place as nice as this need so much security?

We motor down the smooth driveway towards three massive buildings surrounding a perfectly manicured lawn. In my mind's eye, I can picture kids hanging out here, chucking Frisbees, and relaxing on the grass. Except, at this early hour there's no one around. Which reminds me I don't want to get a sunburn.

Crawler pulls around the circular driveway and parks in front of the center building. As I remove my helmet and step out of the sidecar, I can only marvel at the gigantic structure before me. The building is five stories high and half a mile long. The exterior is red brick, with crisp white windows, and a cupola adorning the roof. The giant, double-doored entrance is flanked by marble white columns. I've got to admit, this place is downright swanky.

"What do you think?" Crawler asks.

"I suppose it's nice," I say, "for a school."

"Glad you like it," Crawler says. "But it's not just any school. Come check it out."

Crawler pushes the doors open with his spider legs, and my eyebrows go up. The entrance hall is simply enormous, maybe bigger than a basketball court, with a giant, iron chandelier hanging over pristine marble floors. Two intricately carved wooden staircases flank the sides, leading several stories high. Perched along the walls are massive, stone statues of creatures with wings that look like gargoyles. I count six in total.

On the back wall hangs a large black banner with a white shield. The inside of the shield is very detailed, almost like a coat of arms, with old-looking symbols and mosaic patterns in the shape of strange creature's heads. Dead center is the school's name—Van Helsing Academy—in bold, gothic type. Beneath the shield is a saying, which reads:

YOU MUST BELIEVE IN THINGS YOU
CANNOT IMAGINE.

Huh? What's that supposed to mean?

"This is the main building," Crawler says. "Our students take all of their classes here. This building also houses the cafeteria, the library, the auditorium, and the gymnasium. Oh, and a pool."

"You have a pool?" I say, almost too excitedly. "I mean, that's very interesting," I say, more matter-of-factly. Honestly, I'm impressed. I've never seen a school as decked out as this one.

Crawler looks amused. "Our faculty wing is also on the ground floor," he says. "Let's head that way. There's someone I'd like you to meet."

As we walk, our footsteps echo through a series of grand, dimly lit hallways. In one, I see a grandfather clock ticking away and check the time. It's four in the morning.

"Are you sure people are up at this hour?" I ask. "It's awfully early."

"Oh, don't worry," Crawler says. "He's up."

He? Who's 'he?'

Several minutes later we enter another wing. A plaque on the wall reads:

FACULTY OFFICES

We pass several closed offices with nameplates posted on the front doors. They read:

PROFESSOR LAWRENCE SEWARD
PROFESSOR QUINCY MORRIS IV
PROFESSOR LUCY HOLMWOOD
PROFESSOR ALASTAIR HEXUM

Strangely, there's one door with several locks and chains on the outside. The nameplate reads:

PROFESSOR CLAUDE FAUSTIUS

But that's not all, hanging from Faustius' doorknob is another sign that reads:

ENTRY FORBIDDEN

Strange.

We keep walking until we reach a final office at the end of the hallway. It's different than the others, with large, black doors and a rounded archway. The nameplate on the door reads:

HEADMASTER LOTHAR VAN HELSING, MD, JD, Ph.D., D. Th., Etc., Etc.

Van Helsing? Hang on. Isn't that the name of the school? Suddenly, my stomach drops. I feel like I'm about to see the principal, except this time I didn't do anything wrong. I mean, I don't even go here.

So why am I so freaked out?

My gut tells me to split, but before I can move, one of Crawler's spindly legs RAPS on the door.

We wait for a response, but there's nothing.

"Shucks," I say. "I guess we should come back another time."

"No, go ahead," Crawler says. "He's in there."

"But nobody answered," I say.

"The door is warm," Crawler says. "He's in there. Good luck."

"Wait," I say, "aren't you coming with me?"

"Uh-uh," Crawler says. "He wants to see you alone."

Of course he does.

"Oh, and get ready," Crawler continues, "it's toasty in there."

Toasty? I grab the doorknob and it's super-warm to the touch. I guess he's not kidding. Well, here goes nothing. I pull open the door and step inside. But instead of entering a room, I find myself standing in a dark corridor.

What's up? Doesn't he pay the electric bill?

Fortunately, my eyes don't need to adjust, but as I turn back to question Crawler's assertion that someone is actually in here, the door slams shut in my face.

Great.

I guess there's only one way to go.

Well, Crawler was right about one thing, it's like a sauna in here! Sweat starts dripping from my body so I pull off my hoodie. I feel a bit cooler in my t-shirt, but I'm still sweating like a pig. Unfortunately, it looks like humidity isn't the only obstacle I'll have to deal with.

That's because this place is a hoarder's dream.

Everywhere I look are books—on shelves, on surfaces, even on the floor. In fact, I've never seen so many books stuffed in one place before. There are thick ones, thin ones, old ones, and really old ones. Well, I can say this about Van Helsing, he's certainly well-read. There's a narrow pathway cutting through the center, just wide enough to squeeze through.

Lucky me.

I make my way forward until the corridor ends in a small room that looks like a mad scientist's lair. Test tubes of various colors line the walls. Microscopes, Bunsen burners, and other scientific equipment cover every square inch of table space. There are all sorts of unfinished inventions scattered about, including a broom attached to some kind of a rocket.

That room then connects to another narrow hallway littered with medieval weaponry. There are swords, and axes, and spears, and all sorts of ancient armor you'd find in a museum or something. I move cautiously, trying not to get diced like an onion.

Finally, I enter a chamber that's considerably more open than the rest. Strangely, it's also way more organized. I see books neatly arranged on shelves, mugs hanging handle-side up, color-coordinated arrows resting in quivers, a raging fire, and…

My heart skips a beat.

A man with piercing blue eyes is staring at me.

His gaze is so intense all I can do is freeze and stare right back. He's bald on top, with long, gray hair falling along the sides and back. While his face is wrinkled and weathered, his body is stocky and strong, with a barrel chest and thick arms. Despite the oppressive warmth, he's sitting by the raging fireplace, bundled up in a sweater, gloves, and a scarf. Yet, he's not sweating at all.

"Welcome, Bram," he says. "Welcome to the Van Helsing Academy."

I'm stunned.

"How do you know my name?" I ask.

"All will be explained in due time," he says. "But first, it would only be polite to introduce myself. I am Headmaster Lothar Van Helsing."

I was right. This is his school. But I can't place his accent. It's not French. Maybe German? Or Dutch?

"Please, join me," he says, beckoning me inside. "We have much to discuss. Including your recent werewolf encounter."

"What do you know about that?" I ask anxiously. "Do you know why they were after me?"

"Indeed, I do," he says. "And I am afraid this is just the beginning. You see, the werewolves are merely pawns of a far greater danger."

A chill runs down my spine. I mean, what could be more dangerous than werewolves?

"But I do not wish to alarm you so soon," he says, offering me a chair across from him. "Please, have a seat. Let us get acquainted."

Okay, everything about this guy has me fairly creeped out, but I need to get answers and he seems like my best bet. So, I sit down across from him.

"Would you care for a beverage?" he asks.

"Yes," I say. "That would be great." My throat is really dry. I could use some water.

He leans towards the fire and scoops a ladle into a cauldron, pouring a steaming red liquid into a teacup. Then, he passes it to me.

"What's this?"

"Frog tea," he says. "It is steeped in the skin of the northern red-legged frog who makes his habitat from British Columbia to Northern California. I made it especially for you."

Did he just say red-legged frog skin? Gross!

"Thanks," I say, putting the cup on the floor. "I think I'll let it cool down first."

"As you wish," he says, taking a sip from his cup. "Ah, delicious. I am sure you have many questions. But first, perhaps you will allow me to begin with a brief history lesson, and then we will discuss how it relates to you."

"Um, sure," I say. Truthfully, history was never my best subject, but I'm willing to see where this goes.

"Excellent," he says. "My tale begins way back in the fifteenth century, where a boy named Vlad Dracul was born to a powerful lord in the ancient land of Sighisoara. Unfortunately, the boy's life was cursed from the start, as his father gave him away as a hostage to appease the Sultan of the Turks who ruled all of the lands."

"Wow, that sounds rough," I say.

"It was," Van Helsing says. "Poor Vlad grew up as a

prisoner, and I will spare you the details, but let us say the Sultan did not treat him well. Around the time Vlad became a young man, the Sultan turned on Vlad's father, destroying his kingdom and leaving Vlad an orphan. From that day forward, Vlad swore he would avenge his family, but it was only a fantasy, as Vlad remained a prisoner for another decade. That is, until one night…"

For some reason, Van Helsing trails off.

"Until one night, what?" I ask, surprising myself by how much I'm into the story.

"Until one night," Van Helsing continues, "a band of his father's loyalists snuck into the Sultan's palace and set Vlad free. They escaped to a land called Wallachia, where Vlad became their ruler. There they built a fortress that became known throughout the land as Castle Dracula."

Castle… Dracula?

"Sorry," I interrupt. "But you just said 'Dracula.' Are you talking about 'the' Dracula? Like, you're saying there was a real Dracula or something?"

"Yes, I am speaking of 'the' Count Dracula," Van Helsing says. "And he was as real as the werewolves you encountered today."

I'm speechless. Is he serious? But then again, if I hadn't seen those werewolves with my own eyes, I'd think he was a crackpot.

"Unfortunately," Van Helsing continues, "Vlad Dracul never got his revenge, because he was killed on the battlefield fighting against the Turks. Rumors of his death, however, seemed greatly exaggerated, because when his grave was exhumed months later, his coffin was found empty."

Empty? Suddenly, my mind races back to that newspaper headline about the grave robbery.

"Stories began to circulate," Van Helsing continues, "that Vlad's followers had used an enchanted artifact known as the Blood Grail to bring Vlad's body back to life, returning him once again to the land of the living, but not as a living being. Instead, Vlad Dracul returned as something else entirely—a vampire—and he took a new name, Count Dracula, the King of Darkness, Lord of the Undead."

Well, this has certainly turned gloomy.

"What do you mean by 'undead?'" I ask.

"The undead are beings who were once deceased," he says, "but are brought back to life."

"Seriously?" I say. "You're saying this is all real?"

"As real as you and me," Van Helsing says.

Van Helsing pauses, not for dramatic effect, but because I probably look like a deer in headlights. I'm also feeling lightheaded.

"Are you okay?" Van Helsing asks. "Perhaps you need some nourishment?"

"Yeah, good idea," I say, picking up the teacup with a shaky hand. I don't want to drink it, but it's my only option. Plus, it's red. That's weird. Does Van Helsing know about my red-food thing, or is it just a coincidence?

I take a sip. Surprisingly, it's good.

"Wow, this doesn't stink."

"Thank you," Van Helsing says with a wink. He raises his cup. "Cheers. Shall I continue?"

"Yes, please," I say, drinking the rest.

"Very well," he continues. "Soon, strange things began happening across the land. People started disappearing in the night, only to return as vampires themselves—servants of Dracula's ever-expanding army of the undead. He was unstoppable, rumored to possess remarkable powers: shapeshifting, mind control, super strength, super speed, the power to control vermin, and an unrelenting thirst for blood. But even with all of this, his most dangerous asset remained his mind."

Van Helsing stops momentarily and takes another sip. I'm on the edge of my seat waiting for him to continue.

"You see," Van Helsing says finally, "Count Dracula was as ambitious in death as he was in life. He was a conqueror by nature, and his desire for power was unrelenting. But he also learned his new form had weaknesses. For example, he could not operate in daylight or pass over bodies of water. But most of all, he was afraid of dying again."

Can't blame him there. I'm not a fan of dying myself.

"Not willing to risk himself," Van Helsing continues, "he operated only in the night. But with rapid changes in science and technology, he needed allies to help him conquer the world and keep his operation moving during the day. So, he amassed a cult of human followers to assist him. He promised them riches, land, and power. They called themselves the Dark Ones."

For some reason, I shudder. Why would humans help Dracula? At first, I can't think of any logical reasons, but then I remember all of the power-hungry people I've met in my life, like Glume and Snide, and I realize maybe it's not so far-fetched after all.

"But there were always forces to oppose them," Van Helsing says. "My ancestors were at the forefront of those battles, fighting for the lives of the living over the undead. And as recently as a hundred years ago, they believed they had finally defeated Count Dracula and his minions once and for all. But they were wrong."

Van Helsing looks into the fire.

"The Dark Ones are on the rise again," he says. "But no longer just in Europe. Now they are emerging here, in the United States. And they are building strength rapidly."

Hold on. The Dark Ones are here in America? That doesn't sound good, but there's something I still don't understand, so I just blurt it out.

"Look, this is an incredibly disturbing story, but I still don't understand what it has to do with me?"

"Is it not obvious, Bram?" Van Helsing says, leaning towards me, the fire crackling in his eyes.

"You are the last vampire."

CHAPTER FIVE

THIS MUST BE A JOKE

"**U**m, do you mind going over that last part again?" I ask. "Because I think you just mistakenly called me a vampire."

Now I've been called plenty of things in my life, but 'vampire' has never been one of them. At this point, I'm totally doubting Van Helsing's sanity, but he just leans back in his chair and smiles. There's a twinkle in his eye, like he was expecting me to react like this.

What's his problem?

"I understand why you are surprised," he says. "After all, vampires are horrible creatures. But trust me when I tell you there is no mistake. You *are* a vampire. Would you like me to prove it to you?"

Prove it? I don't know what kind of 'proof' he's got, so this should be entertaining. I nod my approval.

"Very well," he says. "Let us begin with your physical characteristics. They are not as pronounced as other vampires I have seen before you, but all of the key markers are there, though more subtly. For example, you possess the trademark dark hair and dark eyes of a vampire, but one could argue those features are commonplace among the general population. However, if I go a level deeper, the upper helix of your ear has a pronounced point, but not so much as to seem unusual to the untrained eye. Similarly, the canine teeth of your upper jaw are ever-so-slightly elongated, but again this would not appear as meaningful to the unsuspecting."

I pinch the point on my right ear and suddenly feel self-conscious. Yeah, I noticed that stuff about me too, but I didn't think it qualified me as a vampire.

"Then, there is the matter of your skin tone," he continues, "which is as pale as bone. This complexion is quite rare amongst the general population, but a telling feature amongst vampires. Of course, this paleness has an unfortunate side effect. You burn easily when directly exposed to sunlight."

Now I realize I'm rubbing my left arm. Okay, he nailed that one. This Van Helsing guy is crazy observant.

"Let us move on to your behavioral characteristics," he says, "which I believe will be far more revealing. For the sake of expediency, I will summarize them. You have more energy at night than during the day, at times you can move at remarkable speed, you can see perfectly in the dark, and you only crave food that is red in color. That last one is novel even for me, but it still fits the overall pattern."

"Which is?" I ask.

"Vampires feed on blood," Van Helsing says. "And as you know, blood is red."

Whoa! Is that why I only eat red things? Because I'm … a vampire?

I feel the sudden urge to throw up.

"In addition," he continues, "we have recently learned you can communicate with rats, yet another telltale characteristic of a vampire. By the way, those rats you conversed with in the group home dungeon are the very reason you were identified by Dracula's minions in the first place."

"Wait, you mean those rats were real?"

"Quite real," he says. "You should note that rats are generally a disloyal lot. Those two sold their information directly to the Dark Ones and were handsomely rewarded. Have I succeeded in convincing you yet?"

Unfortunately, I can't argue with anything he's told me. Then, a strange thought crosses my mind.

"But if I'm a vampire, how come I'm not sucking people's blood?"

"An excellent question," Van Helsing says. "Perhaps now is the appropriate time to discuss your lineage. But before we do, it is important to remember that numerous tales have been told about Count Dracula, but I can assure you they are all just fiction. What I am about to share with you is the cold-hearted truth."

What does that mean? But I'll have to wait as Van Helsing takes another sip of his frog brew. Meanwhile, my mind flashes through all of the pop culture references I know about Dracula. The movies, the comic books, the novels. I know they're only stories, but they all have one thing in common—Count Dracula is always pure evil.

Van Helsing finishes his drink and begins again. "In the world of the Supernatural, you may be surprised to learn that you come from royalty. You see, your great-grandparents, Jonathan and Mina Harker, played a central role in the downfall of Count Dracula himself, but not before suffering greatly at the hands of the fiend."

Great-grandparents? I've never heard of any great-grandparents.

"The time," Van Helsing continues, "was the late nineteenth century, and Count Dracula was looking to exert an even greater influence over the world. To accomplish this, he moved his base of operations from the remote wilderness of Wallachia to London, a densely populated city where he could easily add unfortunate victims to his undead army. Before long, his forces swelled and the city was in complete disarray. Dracula's victory over humanity would have been assured had he not met your great-grandmother."

His statement shocks me. What did my great-grandmother have to do with this?

"Mina was bright and attractive," Van Helsing says, "and Dracula took a special interest in her, so much so that he did not turn her into a vampire with just one bite. Unbeknownst to Mina, the villain visited her repeatedly during the night, preying upon her, taking his time in transforming her into one of his loyal, undead subjects. That is, until his actions were discovered by your great-grandfather."

"What did he do?" I ask, fascinated.

"Jonathan Harker was a brave man," Van Helsing continues, "and when Mina's behavior grew odder and odder, he realized something was wrong. Soon, he uncovered Count Dracula's nefarious plot but could do nothing to stop the monster. Jonathan, however, would not give up until he found a way to save his beloved wife. He searched frantically, sending letters around the globe until he found a Dutch man with intimate knowledge of how to destroy Dracula. That man was my grandfather, Abraham Van Helsing, an expert in all things Supernatural."

"Hold the phone," I say. "Are you saying my ancestors knew your ancestors?"

"Indeed," Van Helsing says. "And if it weren't for the combined daring of those two men, your great-grandmother would have succumbed to Dracula's power, and the world would have plunged into darkness. But under the tutelage of my grandfather, Jonathan Harker did the impossible. He destroyed Count Dracula. And once Dracula was vanquished, his army of the undead turned to dust. Fortunately, Mina had not been transformed into a vampire, and upon Dracula's demise, she reverted to her natural state. She was saved."

"So, she lived a normal life?" I ask.

"For a while," Van Helsing says. "But then things took a turn for the worse. As you can imagine, news of Count Dracula's 'death' swept far and wide. Your great-grandparents wanted to live a quiet life, but instead, they became unwilling celebrities across all of Europe. And while some still believed Dracula was only a character in a bedtime story, the Dark Ones knew the truth, and they sought revenge against Jonathan and Mina."

"What kind of revenge?" I ask, cringing.

"The worst kind of revenge," Van Helsing says. "But fortunately, they failed, and Jonathan and Mina realized they were no longer safe in Europe. With the help of my grandfather, they changed their names to Joseph and Miriam Murray and booked passage to America to start life anew. But even in the new world, they could not escape the curse of Count Dracula."

"Why not?" I ask.

"Because it was always with them," Van Helsing responds. "You see, while Mina, now called Miriam, had never transformed into a full vampire, she had come so dangerously close that unbeknownst to them, her blood had been forever contaminated. She was now the only surviving carrier of the vampire pathogen—a virus she passed down to your grandfather, and then to your father, and now to you. By blood, your ancestors were half-vampire, and so are you."

Half-vampire?

I'm half-vampire?

"Y-You're kidding?" I stammer.

It's strange to even think about, but deep down I know it's true. And then it hits me. Maybe what Snide said about my father is also true. Suddenly, I feel angry.

"It figures my father was part vampire," I say. "He never loved me. He abandoned me."

"That is partially true," Van Helsing says. "Your father abandoned you, but he did it because he loved you."

"That's a lie!" I yell, surprising myself by my reaction. "How could anyone abandon someone they love?"

"To save your life," Van Helsing says. "Your father was stubborn, but he was a good man who valued your life more than his own."

"What are you saying?" I ask. "You're talking like you

knew him."

"That is because I did know him," Van Helsing says. "Your father, Gabriel Murray, was once a student here."

What? Now my mind is blown. My father was a student here? At the Van Helsing Academy? I thought there couldn't be any more shocking news about my life, but it just keeps on coming. Then, I realize he said my father's last name was Murray. But my last name is Matthews?

"Hold on," I say. "Gabriel Murray. Jonathan and Mina Murray. Are you saying my real last name isn't Matthews? It's … Murray?"

"Yes," Van Helsing says. "Your given name is Abraham Murray. Your father was one of my very first students. His parents had passed away, and he was on his own then. Just a teenager—a lost soul. He had no idea how special he was."

Van Helsing looks longingly into the fire.

"What do you mean?" I ask.

"In the beginning," he says, "this school was intended for Natural students. We did not teach the things we do now. We did not have to. But when I discovered Gabriel, I realized the Supernatural world of my grandfather was still very much alive, and I knew it was my duty to help your father. Your father was our first Supernatural student and he had the spirit of a wild horse. Gabriel knew he was different from the others, but I never told him why. The Dark Ones were non-existent in America, and since there was no imminent danger, I decided he was better off not knowing his true heritage."

"Wait, you never told him he was half-vampire?"

"No," Van Helsing says. "And as he grew into a young adult, he began feeling confined behind our gates. He became increasingly rebellious, challenging the way we did things. He called this place a prison and demanded to leave. I tried to convince him to stay, for his own safety. But he did not understand and one night he ran away. I never saw him again."

I see the sadness in his eyes.

"We... I... lost track of him," Van Helsing says. "At the time I did not have the resources to find him. It was only through a chance encounter with an old colleague that I learned what had happened to Gabriel. He had gone far away, met a Natural girl, and fell in love. He got a job, they married, bought a house. Life was normal for a while."

"That's good, right?" I ask.

"Yes, of course," Van Helsing says. "I wanted him to be happy with his choices. But, unfortunately, it did not last. At that time the Dark Ones were returning to prominence in Europe. Employing new methods, they retraced Count Dracula's final steps, leading to the mysterious disappearance of your great-grandparents. They discovered Jonathan and Mina's new identities, followed their path to America, and tracked down their descendants. By the time we figured out what was happening, the Dark Ones had discovered your parents and... we were too late. They perished in a terrible fire."

I had always been told that's how they died. I just never knew the story behind it.

Van Helsing looks down and I can see he feels horrible. Like it was his fault.

"From that point forward," Van Helsing says, "I changed everything. I dedicated my life to protecting those who could not protect themselves—Supernatural children. They were innocent outcasts in society, abandoned by their very own families. They were labeled as monsters and left to survive on their own, hunted by human predators who wanted to destroy them."

I'm shocked. I had no idea all of that was happening. I mean, I've survived pretty much on my own, but I never had people hunting me down.

"My academy became a haven for these special children," Van Helsing says. "A place where they could master their gifts while defending themselves against the prejudices of the Natural world. And one day, they will be called upon to save those who shunned them."

Wow. If that's what this school is about it's kind of inspiring.

"But despite our success," Van Helsing continues, "we still did not have the means to defeat a nebulous organization like the Dark Ones. And then, one day, our network provided intelligence that a child with strikingly similar characteristics to Gabriel was discovered in foster care. And that child was you."

For some reason, I feel tingly all over.

"I realized that, in some way, my training had paid off," Van Helsing continues. "Your father must have sensed danger and placed you into foster care, giving you a new last name to conceal your identity. It was likely his final act before facing the Dark Ones."

I'm stunned. So, my father didn't abandon me? He put me in foster care to save me? Then, I have a strange thought. What about my mom? Did she know who my father was? Did she know he put me in foster care?

"Did you know my mom?" I ask.

"No, I never had the pleasure," Van Helsing says. "But now we knew of you."

I'm confused. "So, if you knew I was out there, why didn't you bring me here? Like all of those other kids you were talking about."

"Because you were different. It was clear from the beginning that you shared the same restless spirit as your father. Vampires are notoriously independent, and I swore I would not make the same mistake twice. It was a difficult decision, but I feared if I brought you here too young, you would grow to resent it, just like your father. So, instead, we kept a careful watch on you."

Whoa! What? Suddenly, I'm red hot.

"You mean you decided to let me suffer out there?" I say, my voice rising. "You just sat here and watched me burn through all of those foster families? All of that bullying? And you didn't even have the decency to tell me who or what I really was?"

"Yes," Van Helsing says. "I decided it was best for you to live free for as long as you could. To experience the world your father longed for. I do not regret this decision."

"I do!" I say. "I can't believe this."

"I understand your outrage," Van Helsing says. "But the timing was not right. Now things are different. The Dark Ones will not stop until they bring Dracula back."

"Bring him back?" I say. "How's that possible? I thought you said he was destroyed."

"Only his mortal body was destroyed," Van Helsing says. "But his soul is immortal. The Dark Ones are working to bring him back to life, and they might succeed if they find the Blood Grail."

"What's a Blood Grail?" I ask, remembering Van Helsing mentioning it before.

"It is the cursed artifact that brought Count Dracula into existence in the first place. If the Dark Ones find it, they may be able to resurrect him once again. It is up to us to stop them."

"Us?" I say. "Hang on a second, I didn't sign up for this. I didn't say I'd help you."

"I know I have shared a lot," Van Helsing says. "Most of which is a surprise to you. But remember, if the Dark Ones succeed, Count Dracula will ravage America and everything we know will be in peril. You must join us, Bram."

"I don't have to do anything," I say. "On second thought, I think I will do something. I'm getting the heck out of here."

I stand up and head for the exit.

"Bram, wait," Van Helsing says. "You are making a mistake. It is dangerous out there. The werewolves work for the Dark Ones and they will pursue you relentlessly. We can train you here. We can teach you how to use your abilities. There are other students here who—"

But I never hear Van Helsing's last words because I'm gone, squeezing my way out of his cluttered office. Once outside, I take a deep breath. My head is throbbing and my clothes are dripping with sweat. Man, it feels good to get out of there.

This whole thing is nuts. I mean, what's wrong with that guy? He knew everything about my life but chose not to tell me about it. Who does that?

Anyway, I was expecting Crawler to be waiting for me, but he's not around. I don't know how long I was in Van Helsing's office, but now the sun is up. I'm tired and hungry, but I've got to keep moving. I need to get as far away from this place as possible.

I retrace my steps as best as I can remember, sprinting past the faculty doors—all still closed—and turning down a long hallway. I run through a bunch of corridors hoping to find the front entrance, but instead, I wander into a large space that looks like a gym.

Standing in the center is a girl. She's walking in the opposite direction, but maybe she knows the way out.

"Excuse me," I call out.

The girl turns around, and I hate to admit it, but she kind of takes my breath away. She's really pretty, with bright blue eyes and long brown hair. She's wearing a black sweater with some kind of a silver badge on it.

"Yeah?" she says. "Do I know you?"

"W-Well, no," I stammer. "But I—"

Just then I notice a huge block hanging by a thin rope from the ceiling, about fifty feet high in the air. How did I miss that? It looks like it weighs a ton and it's hovering right over her head. Does she even know it's there? I mean, if that thing drops, she'll be crushed!

"Do you need something?" she asks, putting a hand on her hip. "Because I'm kind of busy right now."

I'm about to answer, when…

The rope snaps.

CLASSIFIED

Person(s) of Interest

CODE NAME: HEADMASTER

REAL NAME: LOTHAR VAN HELSING

BASE OF OPERATIONS: VAN HELSING ACADEMY

FACTS: Van Helsing is the third generation in a family of infamous monster hunters. Van Helsing founded the Van Helsing Academy to harbor and train Supernatural children. The purpose of this training is unknown. He is under constant surveillance.

FIELD OBSERVATIONS:

- Carries a silver crossbow
- Dresses in winter clothing, regardless of the season
- Exceptionally intelligent and evasive

Category: Natural

Sub-Type: Not Applicable

Height: 5'11"

Weight: 215 lbs

STATUS: ACTIVE TARGET

DEPARTMENT OF SUPERNATURAL INVESTIGATIONS

CHAPTER SIX

TALK ABOUT EMBARRASSING

"Look out!" I yell, pointing up.

The blue-eyed girl stares at me quizzically, but when she looks up her expression changes to horror as she sees the massive block falling over her head. She's about to be squished like a grape!

Without thinking, I launch into action.

I race towards her, kicking into super speed mode, everything around me moving in slow motion. I'm not sure where I'm getting this extra energy from because I thought I didn't have anything left.

But I can't figure it out now, because if I mistime this rescue by even a fraction of a second, we'll both be pancakes.

As I peek up, the block is halfway there and the girl is reeling back in shock, her brown hair bouncing dramatically like she's in a shampoo commercial.

This is gonna be close.

Then, everything around me darkens.

I'm right under it!

I might get crushed, but I can't break my stride.

I pump my arms and legs harder.

She's inches away.

I feel the block pressing down on my hair.

It's on top of me!

I reach out to wrap her up, hoping my momentum carries us both out of harm's way.

But I come up empty!

I narrowly clear the block's path before it CRASHES to the gym floor, vaulting me sky high. I land hard on my stomach and get the wind knocked out of me, tumbling head over heels until I smash into a blue-padded wall.

I'm bruised, but that doesn't matter.

What happened to the girl?

She was right in front of me. All I had to do was grab her. There's no way I could have missed.

So, does that mean she's…?

I sit up nervously, fully expecting to find a big, disgusting mess. But there's… nothing? I mean, that big old block is there, sticking halfway out of the gym floor. But there's no girl. Or girl parts.

Holy cow. She must be under the block.

Suddenly, I hear a muffled noise. Strangely, it almost sounds like… giggling? And then, to my astonishment, a figure steps out of the center of the block itself.

My jaw drops.

I-It's the girl!

But instead of walking, she floats in the air straight towards me, hovering a few feet away. Then, she lands gently, her hands on her hips.

It's her! But then I realize she doesn't seem like she's here. I mean, I can actually see right through her, like she's transparent!

"A-Are you an angel?" I ask.

"Nope," she says, "Just your friendly neighborhood ghost."

Wait, did she just say… ghost?

"And by the way," she continues, "I didn't need to be saved. I can take care of myself."

Then, I notice the silver badge on her black sweater. It has a big letter 'M' that looks like it was engraved by the claws of a lion. And there's a word beneath it. It reads:

AURA

"Who's that guy?" comes a boy's voice.

"He ruined everything!" another boy says.

Suddenly, there's a whole group of kids gathered around me. But then I realize they're not kids at all.

They're… monsters?

And all of them are wearing black sweaters, just like the ghost girl, with their own silver badges.

I take in the scene.

To the girl's left is a big kid whose entire body is covered in brown fur. His shaggy face sort of looks like an ape, with a thick brow, small nose, and large jaw. He's not wearing any shoes, and his feet are absolutely enormous. For some reason, he reminds me of Bigfoot, only smaller. His badge says:

HAIRBALL

Behind him is a skinny kid who makes me do a double take. He sort of looks like that fish guy in the Creature from the Black Lagoon movie. He has green scaly skin, black eyes, and large pointy ears. His entire head is encased in a clear, round helmet filled with water, and gill-like flaps are opening and closing on the sides of his neck. His badge reads:

STANPHIBIAN

To the girl's right is a kid wrapped in white bandages from head to toe, except for a giant pair of sunglasses covering his eyes. What's up with this guy? Is he trying to be a mummy or something? Anyway, his badge reads:

INVISIBILL

Finally, a smaller boy with rosy cheeks, messy blond hair, and a worried expression peers cautiously around the bandaged kid. He's wearing blue-rimmed glasses with a cord connected to each earpiece. Compared to the rest of them he looks downright normal. But for some reason his badge says:

RAGE

Rage? Why is that little guy called Rage? And Aura? Hairball? Stanphibian? InvisiBill? Are these their real names?

Strangely, they're all staring at me, like I'm the weird one. Unfortunately, I can't even stand up because I'm totally wiped out. And I still don't know how I managed that last burst of speed considering I'm running on fumes. All I know is that I'm breathing hard and feeling incredibly woozy.

"He ruined everything!" Hairball says.

"Yeah," InvisiBill says. "It took Stanphibian over an hour to get that block up there."

"Two hours," the fish-kid says, with a sad fish face.

"Okay, dude," Aura says. "You ruined our training exercise. Now spill it, who the heck are you?"

"Do you even go here?" Rage asks.

"Of course he doesn't go here, bonehead," Aura says. "He's not wearing a house badge."

"Sorry," I say. "I wasn't trying to ruin anything. I just thought she… she…"

Suddenly, I'm not feeling so good. My skin feels hot like it's on fire. Then, my stomach starts quivering like I'm going to… to…

"Oh god, he's hurling!" Hairball says.

"So nasty!" InvisiBill says, blocking his sunglasses.

"Shut it, you morons," Aura says. "He needs help. Someone get a bucket."

"On it," Rage says, running off.

I don't know what's wrong with me. I'm in a full sweat and my body is shaking like a leaf. Oh no. Not again! Here it—

"Seriously?" Hairball says. "You know, I can't unsee this."

This is so embarrassing, but I can't stop myself.

Finally, Rage shows up with a bucket, pushing it in front of me with his foot.

"Here you go," he says.

"Th-Thanks," I say, wiping my chin. Everything starts spinning and I pull the bucket close.

"You okay?" Aura asks.

"N-N-No," I stammer. Everything is definitely not okay. I close my eyes, but the spinning sensation doesn't stop. In fact, it's only getting worse, like I'm on a roller coaster and can't get off.

When I open my eyes, the kids are still there, but they look like they're upside down. Aura's mouth is moving, but I can't hear what she's saying.

Then, everything goes dark.

***

"He sure doesn't look like a vampire," comes a boy's voice. "He doesn't even have fangs. Aren't vampires supposed to have fangs?"

"His ears are pointy," a girl says. "But I think they're too big for his head."

Now hang on a minute! I don't know who's talking, but I'm not going to just stand here and be insulted. I try opening my eyes, but my head is pounding. Then, I realize I'm not standing at all. I'm lying down on something soft.

Where am I?

Then, I remember. The gymnasium. Those strange kids. Ugh, I must have passed out. As if that whole scene wasn't humiliating enough.

"Still," the boy says. "He doesn't look like a vampire."

"You of all people should know you don't have to look like a monster to be a monster?" the girl says.

"True," the boy says. "But fangs would be cool."

Okay, that's enough. I force my eyes open and, to my surprise, the first thing I see is a red tube sticking out of my arm. What's that? Is someone drugging me?

Instinctively, I reach up to pull it out.

"He's awake!" the girl yells. "Doctor!"

Suddenly, I feel someone pulling my arm back. It's that Rage kid. And Aura is floating behind him.

"Stop it!" Rage yells. "They're feeding you through that tube!"

Feeding me?

"So, you're not drugging me?" I ask.

"No," Rage says. "That tube is pumping tomato puree into your system."

"Oh," I say. "Really? My bad." Wait a minute, how did they know to give me red food?

"Chill, Bram," Aura says. "You're safe here. They know what you need."

"How do you know my name?" I ask.

"Headmaster Van Helsing told us," she says.

Van Helsing? I guess my face betrays me, because then she says, "He's a good man. We know what you're going through and trust us, you're safe here. Okay?"

I don't know why, but when I look into her blue eyes, I feel calmer. Rage lets go of my arm.

"Where am I?" I ask.

"The infirmary," Aura says. "You were in really bad shape, but now you've got a little color in your cheeks, which isn't bad for a vampire."

I must admit I'm feeling a lot better. I guess I pushed myself too hard. I've never felt like that before.

"How's the patient?" comes a woman's voice.

I turn, and my eyes bulge out of their sockets.

A woman with jet black hair, green skin, and a giant wart on her nose is checking my vital signs. She looks like a... a....

"I'm Dr. Hagella," she says. "And yes, I'm a witch. But I'm also a doctor, which technically makes me a witch doctor." She cackles loudly. "I know, it never gets old. How are you feeling, young man?"

"Better," I say, smiling reluctantly.

"Great," Dr. Hagella says, adjusting the feeding tube. "Your blood count was low. Probably because you hadn't eaten for days. You can't go that long without food."

"I wasn't trying to," I say. "It just happened."

"The vampire-side of your physiology requires you to constantly produce red blood cells. When you don't eat, it slows the production of blood cells leading to aplastic anemia, which can cause dizziness, vomiting, and possibly death. So, you'd better make sure you don't skip meals."

Well, I didn't know that. But I guess that explains my delusional state when I was trapped in that dungeon at the New England Home for Troubled Boys.

"Dr. Hagella is the best," Rage says. "She knows everything."

"Thanks, dear," Dr. Hagella says, patting Rage's head. Then, she turns to me and says, "I'm feeding you with enriched tomato puree. It contains additional proteins that should help your bone marrow start producing red blood cells at a faster rate. Now you need your rest. Hint, hint, little monsters, it's time to leave the patient alone. Don't worry, I'll check on him later."

Dr. Hagella scoops up a few papers and leaves.

"Okay, we'll let you rest," Rage says. "We just wanted to make sure you were okay. Aura and I need to head back to Monster House anyway."

"Um, what's Monster House?" I ask.

"It's the name of the Residence Hall," Rage says. "It's where we live."

"Wait," I say. "You guys live here?"

"Yep," Aura says. "The Van Helsing Academy is our school and our home. It's the only place in the world for kids like us."

"And what kinds of kids are those?" I ask.

"Supernatural kids," she says. "Just like you."

"Yeah," Rage says. "Maybe you'll stick around."

"Um, maybe," I say.

"Great," Rage says. "Well, good luck."

"Hope you recover," Aura says. "We'll probably be up all-night practicing that rescue mission you screwed up for us. We have a test on it tomorrow."

"Sorry about that," I say.

"Not as sorry as we are," Aura says. Then, she disappears through the wall.

Rage shrugs his shoulders and walks out the door.

I'm alone. And totally confused.

Maybe I'm dreaming, but even this is too bizarre. I mean, monster kids? And Aura said this place is not just their school, but also their home. I mean, I've lived in houses before, but never one that felt like home.

But I know I can't stay here.

This place just isn't for me.

"Have you forgiven me yet?" comes a man's voice.

Startled, I look up to find Van Helsing standing in the doorway, still wearing his winter gear. The last thing I want to do is talk to him.

"The doctor said I needed rest," I say.

"She is right," Van Helsing says, entering the room anyway. He takes the seat Rage vacated and adds, "She is an expert on monster biology."

Monster biology? Wait a minute!

"Are you calling me a monster?"

"I am," he says. "And you should get used to it. It is what the world outside will come to know you as. You are different, and you will always be different."

"I'm no monster," I say.

"Not in the traditional sense," Van Helsing says. "After all, I do not know many monsters who would try to save the life of an innocent girl. That shows me you are far from a monster at heart. You are a hero."

"A hero?" I scoff. "I'm no hero."

"Helping those that cannot help themselves is the definition of a hero," Van Helsing says. "You acted because you believed Aura needed help, and I am here because I also need your help. And I believe you need mine."

"I don't need anything from you," I say.

"You may not think so," Van Helsing says. "At least not now. But when the Dark Ones come for you, and come for you they will, you may feel differently."

Images of werewolves flash in my brain, and I know

he's right. I mean, what chance do I have out there on my own? I already know the answer.

None.

"Bram," he continues. "I built this place to be a sanctuary for Supernaturals like you. Danger lies outside these walls. There are monsters, but there are also men who behave like monsters. Men who will stop at nothing to destroy you, or to use you to get what they want. Here you will be safe. Here you will learn to master your skills and properly prepare for the war that is coming."

"I don't want to fight in any war," I say.

"Neither do I," Van Helsing says. "But it is an unavoidable war. It is our responsibility to do something about it, not because we can, but because we must. There are far too many innocent lives at stake. But we cannot win this war without you."

"Why not?" I ask. "You're training all these other kids. Why do you need me?"

"Because you are special," Van Helsing says.

"And why is that?" I ask.

"You are the last of the vampires," Van Helsing says. "You bring special skills no one else can duplicate. You are essential to defeating Count Dracula."

"B-But how?" I ask, my heart suddenly racing.

Just then, the monitor over my head starts BEEPING.

"What's happening?" Dr. Hagella asks, rushing in. "Headmaster, are you over-exciting our patient?"

"I am educating our patient," Van Helsing says, standing up. "Bram, I will explain more when you are stronger. But neither of us should forget the Dark Ones are gathering strength as we speak. We cannot sit back and let them take over the world. It is up to us to stop them. We need you on our side. Will you join us?"

Van Helsing looks me in the eyes and extends his hand, and a million things jump into my head at once.

The parents I never knew.

All of my failed foster families.

Johnny and those innocent kids at the group home.

Aura, Rage, and the other strange kids here.

It's a weird feeling. I mean, I've never been wanted before. I've never been part of a team.

But what if I fail?

Well, I guess if I fail, I'll be toast one way or the other. So, what do I have to lose?

I reach out and shake Van Helsing's hand.

"Okay," I say. "Let's give it a shot."

VAN HELSING ACADEMY

STUDENT ASSESSMENT

VITALS:
NAME: Aurelia Spector
EYES: Blue
HAIR: Brown
HEIGHT: 4'8"
WEIGHT: N/A

NOTES: Phases through objects and floats on air. Shows potential for telekinesis. Can't touch physical objects. Purpose as ghost is unknown.

CODENAME: Aura

CLASSIFICATION TYPE:
Spirit — Ghost

SUPERNATURAL ASSESSMENT:

STRENGTH ●○○○○
AGILITY ●●●●○
FIGHTING ●●●○○
INTELLECT ●●●●●
CONTROL ●●●●○

TEACHABLE?	Yes	No
VAN HELSING	●	○
CRAWLER	●	○
HOLMWOOD	●	○
SEWARD	●	○
MORRIS	●	○
HEXUM	●	○
FAUSTIUS	●	○

RISK LEVEL: LOW

CHAPTER SEVEN

THE MONSTROSITIES AND ME

The next morning I'm officially discharged from the infirmary. Dr. Hagella said I looked appropriately pale for a vampire and sent me straight to the admissions office located in the building next door.

As I step onto the quad, the scene is totally different from when I first arrived at the Van Helsing Academy. This time the sun is shining, and dozens of students are walking across the green wearing backpacks and carrying books. If I didn't know better, I'd think I was strolling through the campus of your average, upscale school.

Except, there's one little thing shattering the illusion.

All of the kids are monsters.

Now, for some of the kids, it's not so easy to tell. You really have to look closely to find an unusual feature or two, like claws, horns, or a tail. But for other kids, you know right away they're different.

Very different.

Like the girl running across the green covered head-to-toe in some kind of bluish armor. Or the kid lying on his back who looks like a cross between a boy and a monitor lizard. There's even a guy flying overhead with giant wings.

It dawns on me that if I were anywhere else, I'd have bolted by now. So, I guess I'm getting used to it.

Sort of.

Then, I notice they're all wearing badges like Aura and Rage, but in different colors. Some badges are bronze and others are blue or green. I wonder what the colors mean?

Because the sun is shining, I don't want to linger too long or I'll get a major sunburn. So, per Dr. Hagella's instructions, I follow the driveway to the large building on the right. According to her, this is the Residence Hall where the students live year-round.

The place Rage called 'Monster House.'

As I climb the stone steps, I feel a sense of awe. The group homes I've been crashing in are dumps compared to this place. I mean, the outside has the same pristine, ivy-league feeling as the other buildings, with red brick, white window frames, and perfectly trimmed hedges.

But as I approach the large double doors I stop.

I mean, do I really belong here?

I guess I'll find out. Besides, it's not like I've got anywhere else to go. So, I pull open the large double doors, step inside, and gasp.

The entrance hall is so enormous I think I could fit two group homes inside of it. My eyes wander from the dark wood walls to the white marble floors to the large windows letting in lots of natural light. There's an extra-wide staircase leading upstairs, and the room is outfitted with comfy sofas and chairs. There's also a big bulletin board filled with flyers. I squint to read one. It says:

MOVIE NIGHT DOUBLE FEATURE
TEEN WOLF & TEEN WOLF 2
THIS THURSDAY

Movie night? Okay, I can get used to this! Well, I can say one thing, these students certainly aren't slumming it.

Then, I notice a familiar-looking banner hanging on the back wall. It's the Van Helsing Academy crest with that strange motto:

YOU MUST BELIEVE IN THINGS YOU
CANNOT IMAGINE.

I suppose it makes a little more sense now. To my left is a door with a sign for the Administration Office. Bingo. Well, I guess it's time to make it official. I walk over, step inside, and nearly faint.

Standing behind the counter is the largest "person" I've ever seen. She's bald, with humungous shoulders, and one giant red eye sitting smack in the middle of her forehead. She's wearing a long, blue tunic and bright red lipstick.

I open my mouth to say hello, but no words come out. She must be, like, twenty feet tall. But then I realize she isn't even standing, she's sitting!

The nameplate on the counter reads:

MS. VIOLET CLOPS

MONSTER HOUSE MANAGER

"Alright, stop yer gawkin'," she says, in a surprisingly deep voice. "I can see yer, y'know?"

"I-I'm sorry," I stammer. "I didn't mean... It's just that..."

"Keep your flap shut before yer says somethin' yer gonna regret," she says. "My name's Ms. Clops. But after a week, if I haven't eaten yer, yer can call me 'Vi.' Yer must be Murray, the new kid."

I'm about to tell her my last name is Matthews when I remember it's not. This is going to take some getting used to. Then, she hands me a big yellow envelope that looks like a Tic Tac in her massive mitts.

"Inside is yer room key, class schedule, and student handbook. Now if yer like most kids, yer stick the handbook in yer desk drawer and forget it existed, so let's get two things straight. One, the basement is off limits. Don't forget. I'd hate for yer to be the second kid in Van Helsing Academy history that gets lost forever on some stupid dare. Is that clear?"

"Um, yes," I say, swallowing hard.

"Two," she continues, "Lights out means lights out. There's no scampering around campus after hours like those kids in them wizarding books. If I catch yer, I'll eat yer on the spot. Is that clear?"

"Y-Yes," I say, overwhelmed by all the new info.

My eyes drift back down to her nameplate.

Violet Clops. Vi Clops. Then, it clicks.

Vi-Clops is like Cy-clops. She's a female Cyclops! And an angry one at that.

"Good," she says, pointing at her eye and then back at me, "because I got my eye on yer. And here's yer backpack. It's got all yer need inside, including yer books, pens, and notebooks."

She tosses it like it's weightless, but when I catch it it's so heavy I nearly fall over.

"Now yer may wanna hit the showers before class. A zombie could smell you coming a mile away. Room number thirteen. Up the stairs, third level on the left. Good luck, Murray."

"Er, thanks," I say.

Well, she's frightening.

I head back to the entrance hall and tackle the staircase. A group of students coming down shoot me odd looks, including a girl with a trunk for a nose who whispers, "Pee-ew," to her friend.

Now I'm feeling self-conscious and I realize it's been days since I've showered. Finally, I reach the third-floor landing and hang a left. There's a handwritten sign on the wall that reads:

HOME OF THE MONSTROSITIES.
KEEP OUT!!!
YES, THAT MEANS YOU!

Okay. That doesn't look promising.

For a second, I consider going back downstairs to ask Vi Clops for another room assignment, but that just might give her an excuse to eat me. So, I press on, passing several doors until I hit room number thirteen. I pull out my key when it dawns on me that I've never held one before. I rub my finger along the metal edges.

Funny, I've probably stayed in hundreds of rooms, but no one has actually ever given me a key. I guess this is a major step up.

I unlock the door and push it open, slamming it into the face of some blond-haired kid who was about to exit.

He falls to the ground backward.

Hang on. I know that kid.

It's Rage!

I'm about to tell him how sorry I am when he lowers his arm from his face and I realize something is seriously wrong. He's bent over, breathing heavily like I've clobbered him with a baseball bat. Then, I notice his entire face is… purple?

"Butterflies and puppies," he pants. "Just think about… butterflies and puppies."

"A-Are you okay?" I ask. "I'm so sorry." I have no idea what's going on. But by the color of his face, it looks like he's going to self-combust or something.

"Butterflies…," he says, breathing in and out slowly. "Just think… happy thoughts."

"Um, maybe I should come back later," I say, backing into the hallway.

"N-No," Rage says, waving his arm. "Come in. I-I'm good. I'm good."

I step inside as Rage gets to his feet. He leans over a chair, catching a second wind. He's sweating profusely, but his face looks like it's back to its natural coloring.

"I'm so sorry," I say. "I was told this was my room."

Then, I notice it's a double. There are two beds, two dressers, and two desks.

"I guess we're going to be roommates," I say.

"Really?" he says. "That's great news! When I first got here, they told me I couldn't have a roommate. I guess I've gotten better."

Oookaaaayyy. What's that supposed to mean?

"That's your half," he says, pointing to my left. "I tried to keep it neat, just in case they changed their minds. My side looks like a train wreck. Sorry."

"No problem," I say, sitting on my bed. Well, he's right about the train wreck part. While my side is empty, his side is an absolute disaster zone. His bed is unmade, his clothing is strewn all over the floor, and his books are scattered everywhere. I wonder if Van Helsing gave him decorating tips.

"Can I see your class schedule?" Rage asks.

"What schedule?" Then I realize it's probably in the envelope Vi Clops 'the boy-eating monster' gave me. I open it up and pull out a bunch of papers. One of them looks like a class schedule, so I hand it to him.

"Interesting," he says, studying it intently. "We're in the same section. That's pretty surprising since they usually group kids by skill level and you haven't even been assessed yet. Oh well. Here you go." Then, he hands it back to me.

I look at it, fully expecting to see the usual subjects like Math and Social Studies, but this class schedule isn't like any schedule I've seen before. It reads:

MONSTEROLOGY 101	09:00
SUPERNATURAL HISTORY 101	10:30
PARANORMAL SCIENCE 101	13:00

SURVIVAL SKILLS I   16:30

"What's with the weird timings," I ask.

"It's a Van Helsing thing," Rage says. "He likes to use military timing."

"Well, these classes certainly look interesting," I say.

"They are," Rage says, "but the teachers are really tough. Especially Hexum. He teaches Survival Skills. I thought I'd die in his class like, five times."

I wait for him to laugh, but I realize he's serious.

Then, I notice the clock. It reads: 8:23 AM.

If I'm going to de-stink before our first class at nine, I'll need to shower now.

"Hey, where's the bathroom?" I ask. "I'd love to shower and feel like a normal person again. Well, sort of normal, I guess."

"Down the hall and to the right," he says. "But you'd better hurry. Oh, hang on." Then, he races to his closet. "Here's one of my towels. I just did laundry so it's clean. And here's a fresh bar of soap and some shampoo."

"Gee, thanks," I say, taking the toiletries. Then I realize I don't have any clothes to change into. "Ugh, I guess I'll have to put these back on afterwards."

"No, wait," he says excitedly, digging into his dresser. "I wondered why all this stuff showed up last night. Now it makes sense. It was way too big for me, so they must have left it for you."

He hands me a pile of clothes. There's a shirt, pants, socks, and clean underwear. I've never been so happy to see clean underwear in my entire life.

"Thanks," I say.

"You better be fast," Rage says. "You've only got about fifteen minutes. Oh, and look out for InvisiBill, he likes to play practical jokes."

I don't know what that means, but I grab all of the stuff and head for the shower.

***

Let me tell you, there's nothing better than a warm shower after spending days caked in your own sweat. I can't remember the last time I felt so clean. I probably stayed in there longer than I should have, but the water felt great against my skin, and I really needed it.

What I don't need, however, is to be late for my very first class. I dry off quickly, and for the first time in a long time, I'm feeling surprisingly optimistic. Despite all of the craziness, maybe this will work out after all.

Then, I rip open the shower curtain and realize something is wrong.

My clothes are missing.

What happened to my clothes?

I know I set them down on the bench right outside the shower. They couldn't have walked off on their own.

Then, I remember Rage's warning.

InvisiBill.

Wait a minute.

Invisi – Bill?

As in, 'Invisible?'

Seriously? That kid with the sunglasses must be invisible under all those bandages! He must have snuck in here and stolen all of my clothes. There's no way I'll make it to class on time now. So much for feeling optimistic.

"Hey!" I call out. "InvisiBill! Bring my stuff back!"

But there's no answer.

I bet that jerk is having the time of his life right now, laughing at my expense.

I don't know what to do. If I use my super speed, I can probably make it back to my room before anyone notices. But then I'll have to put my old, stinky clothes back on.

I call out again, but InvisiBill still doesn't show up.

There's no choice, I'll have to go for it. I tighten the towel around my waist and throw open the bathroom door. Only to find—

"Surprise!" comes a chorus of voices.

Rage is standing there, along with Stanphibian, Hairball, and... Aura! They're all grinning ear to ear.

This is so embarrassing.

Then, to their right, I see my clothes!

They're floating in mid-air.

"Is this a bad time?" Hairball asks.

I'm so humiliated I don't know what to say.

"When you attend the Van Helsing Academy," Aura says, "you're taught to believe in things you can't imagine. That means you can't let your guard down. Not even in the shower. It could mean the difference between life and death."

"I tried to warn you," Rage says.

He warned me, but he could've been more specific.

"Don't be angry at Rage," Aura says. "Let's just say you've been taught your first lesson. You'd better learn it fast if you want to join the Monstrosities."

"What are 'the Monstrosities?'" I ask.

"Not 'what,'" Aura says, "but 'who.' We're the Monstrosities. It's the name of our section. We consider ourselves to be the best of the best. But just because you're in our section doesn't mean you're one of us. You've got to prove yourself first. So, I guess we'll see what you're made of. InvisiBill, give him his clothes back."

Suddenly, my clothes come flying at me. I catch them all, nearly dropping my towel in the process.

"And you get one of these," Rage says, putting a black sweater on top of my pile. It's just like the sweaters they're wearing, but without a badge.

"Silver badges are for Monstrosities only," Aura says. "If you want one, you've got to earn one. Got it?"

"Yep," I say. Although I have a distinct feeling that's not going to be so easy.

"By the way," Rage says. "The closet in our room is filled with new clothes for you."

"Of course it is," I say.

"See you in class," Aura says. "And don't be late. Detention is with Headmaster Van Helsing himself."

VAN HELSING ACADEMY

STUDENT ASSESSMENT

VITALS:
NAME: Billy Griffin
EYES: Unknown
HAIR: Unknown
HEIGHT: 4'10"*
WEIGHT: 90 lbs*
* Estimates

NOTES: Lives in a constant state of invisibility. Casts no shadows. Can be tracked by scent. Is unable to revert back to visible state.

CODENAME: InvisiBill

CLASSIFICATION TYPE:
Abnormal — Invisible

SUPERNATURAL ASSESSMENT:

STRENGTH	●○○○○
AGILITY	●●●●○
FIGHTING	●●○○○
INTELLECT	●●○○○
CONTROL	●○○○○

TEACHABLE?	Yes	No
VAN HELSING	●	○
CRAWLER	○	●
HOLMWOOD	●	○
SEWARD	●	○
MORRIS	●	○
HEXUM	○	●
FAUSTIUS	○	●

RISK LEVEL: MEDIUM

[93]

CHAPTER EIGHT

A CRASH COURSE IN VAMPIRE

Thanks to my super speed, I make it to class with seconds to spare. That was fast, but I realize even faster that my education at the Van Helsing Academy is going to be unlike anything I've ever experienced before.

Case in point, my first class is Monsterology, the study of monsters, taught by Professor Lucy Holmwood, a middle-aged woman with green eyes, red hair, and an unusually cheery disposition given the macabre nature of her subject matter. It takes me a few minutes to get used to her English accent—I mean, is 'gobsmacked' really a word? But as soon as she launches into the four categories of monsters, I'm hooked.

The first group she describes are shapeshifters, which are creatures who can take on other forms. There are two types of shapeshifters: lycanthropes and doppelgangers.

Lycanthropes turn into monsters when naturally occurring events happen, like full moons. Werewolves are the most popular type of lycanthropes, but other 'were' creatures are known to exist, like wererats for instance.

Yep, you heard me. I said wererats.

The other type of shapeshifter is a doppelganger. This creature replicates the exact physical and vocal characteristics of someone else. Professor Holmwood explains that doppelgangers are rare and there are several sub-types although none have been seen in the last century. But then again, how would anyone know for sure?

The next category is spirits. Spirits were once living people whose souls never moved on to their next destination. Now they just hang around, haunting the living. In fact, some spirits don't even know they're dead—talk about awkward conversations! Spirits come in two types: ghosts and skin-riders.

Ghosts are exactly what you think they are, bodiless souls that can drift through walls, windows, and your local McDonalds. Typically, they're stuck here for a reason, but whatever that reason is, it's usually a mystery to them.

A skin-rider, on the other hand, is a nastier kind of spirit. They're stuck between worlds like ghosts, but they can possess the body of a living person, using them to carry out devious deeds, like monopolizing your video game console.

The third category of monsters is the undead. These are the ones Van Helsing talked about earlier. These fun-suckers were once dead, but now they're back alive again.

This group includes all of your Halloween favorites, like vampires, mummies, and zombies. No need to go into the gory details, we know these guys all too well.

The fourth and final group are the abnormals. Abnormals are a catch-all category for anything that can't be classified into one of the previous buckets. In here you'll find your one-of-a-kind beasts, science experiments gone wrong, and bizarre freaks of nature. Think Frankenstein, Godzilla, or the Blob.

It's not until the bell rings that I'm able to put down my pen. I've never taken so many notes in my life! It seems like the ninety minutes flew by in a snap, and I can't believe everything I just learned. Apparently, there's a whole secret monster world out there I never knew existed—and a rather frightening one at that.

But before I can process it all we're off to Supernatural History. With the word 'history' in it, I thought it would be a real snoozer, but boy was I wrong. The class is taught by Professor Lawrence Seward, a heavy-set man with a thick, handlebar mustache. With his red bowtie and tan duster jacket, it looks like he fell out of a 1920s photograph.

Professor Seward starts lecturing before we even take our seats, sending everyone scrambling for their notebooks. And what he's teaching is simply incredible. I had no idea how far back monster history went. Van Helsing told me the whole vampire thing started in the fifteenth century, and I thought that was old. But according to Professor Seward, monsters have been running around for ages.

I learn about the Zombie Crusades of the 1100s, the Werewolf Inquisition of the 1200s, and even the Ghost Rebellion during the Revolutionary War. They never taught us this stuff in public school!

Then, Professor Seward sidetracks into a discussion about Supernatural items. Apparently, certain household items have powerful effects on certain monsters. For example, silver destroys werewolves, salt repels spirits, and garlic can hold a vampire at bay. I guess the trick is remembering not to spray garlic on a werewolf or throw salt at a vampire.

Then, Professor Seward offers bonus points for anyone who can answer questions about ancient Supernatural artifacts, like:

"What is the Spear of Darkness?"

"When would you use Holy Water?"

"What is the Crossbow of Purity?"

Of course, I'm clueless, but Aura's hand shoots up after every question. I have to admit I'm impressed. This girl definitely has game. Then, Professor Seward asks a question that really gets my attention.

"What is the legend of the Blood Grail?"

The Blood Grail? I remember Van Helsing talking about the Blood Grail. The Dark Ones are searching for it. Of course, Aura is all over it.

"According to legend," she begins, "during the War

of the Turks, King Vlad Dracul of Wallachia knew his armies were far out-numbered by his Turkish enemies and were likely to be destroyed. Trapped in a narrow mountain chasm, the King bled a quart of his blood into an empty wine chalice and had his sorcerers perform an ancient spell over it."

Whoa! Van Helsing didn't give me that kind of detail. No wonder it's called the Blood Grail.

"Then," she continues, "Vlad Dracul ordered a contingent of his best men to take the chalice and sneak through enemy lines, returning it safely to his kingdom in Wallachia without spilling a single drop. In the darkness of night, the men did just as the King instructed. And the very next day, just as Dracul predicted, his forces were overrun, and he was killed on the battlefield."

Well, most of that matches up to what I was told.

"But before the Turks could claim his body," Aura continues, "his loyal subjects retrieved his remains and returned them to Wallachia. There, they collected the chalice—now called the Blood Grail—and poured King Dracul's blood over his lifeless body, miraculously returning him to life from the dead. From that moment forward, he became known as Count Dracula, King of Darkness, and Lord of the Undead."

So that's the legend of the Blood Grail, huh? And to think, the Dark Ones are out there looking for it right now. I hope it's smashed into so many pieces Gorilla Glue couldn't put it back together.

After class, we break for lunch. As I enter the cafeteria, I'm shocked to discover dozens of tiny winged creatures with pointy ears and horns on their heads fluttering all over the place. One of them lands on a table and picks up a dirty fork with both hands.

"Imps," Rage says. "They work in the cafeteria. But look out, they like to play pranks. Last week they put strawberry jelly on my hamburger instead of ketchup. I nearly barfed."

"Great," I say.

I move through the buffet looking at all of the options. There's more food here than I've seen in my entire life, including chicken, steak, salads, and sandwiches, but nothing for me. Then, at the end of the line, I see something bright red. It's pizza but without the cheese! I grab a few slices when one of the imps comes flittering around the corner with a large silver shaker that says: Red Pepper Flakes.

Before I can react, it hovers over my pizza and turns the shaker over. But before the flakes hit my food, Rage sticks his hand over my plate.

"Yuck!" Rage says, smelling the specks on his palm. "These aren't red pepper flakes. They're chopped liver flakes. Now shoo."

The imp sticks out its tongue and flies away.

"Thanks," I say.

"Told ya," Rage says. "Now I've got to wash my hands."

When he comes back, we sit together in the crowded cafeteria. Hairball and Rage have steaks larger than their heads, Stanphibian slurps some algae concoction through a straw, and we're all forced to watch InvisiBill chew his chicken fingers into mush before swallowing them down his invisible gullet.

But Aura isn't eating anything at all. She's just sitting there, watching us with her sad, blue eyes.

"Aren't you hungry?" I ask.

"Nope," she says, pushing back her hair. "Ghosts don't get hungry."

Suddenly, it hits me. All of those monster classifications I just learned about apply to us as well! Which means—

"S-So, you're, like, dead?"

"I suppose," she says casually. "I don't remember much about it. Headmaster Van Helsing has been trying to help me figure out what happened. Just like Professor Holmwood said, I'm probably still here for a reason. I just don't know what it is."

"Wow," I say. "I'm sorry."

"Don't be," she says. "It happens to everyone eventually. My turn just came a little early."

I manage to smile, but I feel terrible for her. I mean, she looks like she had everything going for her: smarts, good looks, confidence. Yet, here she is—or isn't.

After lunch, we have Paranormal Science with Professor Quincy Morris IV. He's an athletic-looking man with white, slicked-back hair and a nasty scar running from his forehead down to his chin. He speaks with a thick southern accent, and uses phrases like: "over yonder," "fixin' to," and "y'all."

Today's lesson is all about conducting Supernatural crime scene investigations, and we spend most of our time learning how to properly secure a crime scene. According to Professor Morris, the biggest problem isn't the crime itself, but keeping first responders off the scene. You see, in normal crime situations, firemen, paramedics, and police officers are essential to solving the case, but in a Supernatural crime scene, they typically end up ruining all the evidence.

That's when Professor Morris introduces a lollipop-looking device called a Hypno-Wipe. Under its power, you can hypnotize a whole bunch of people at once, which is great for lots of purposes, like helping them forget everything they just saw. Professor Morris lets us practice using it, which leads to some good laughs, like when Rage hypnotizes Hairball into thinking he's a grizzly bear.

After that, Professor Morris lets us play with a Spirit Sensor. The Spirit Sensor looks just like a watch, but it's really a GPS for tracking ghosts. Professor Morris explains that in most Supernatural crime scenes ghosts are often your best witnesses. The Spirit Sensor detects the presence of ghosts in the area by measuring molecular disturbances. All ghosts have a unique molecular signature. The Spirit Sensor reads that signature and matches it to the appropriate ghost.

Thanks to Aura, we get to try it out firsthand. Professor Morris gives her a five-minute head start and then turns it on, leading to an hour-long ghost chase through the entire building. Every time we think we have her cornered, she just laughs and phases through another wall. That girl is way too competitive.

Unfortunately, the fun and games eventually come to an end, because the bell RINGS and class is over.

Next up is Survival Skills.

"Get ready," Rage warns.

"For what?" I ask.

"For anything," he answers. "Hexum is a mentalist."

"What's that?" I ask.

"You'll see," he says.

To my surprise, Survival Skills isn't taught in a classroom, but in the gymnasium, which looks dramatically different from when I saw it a few days ago. Instead of a large, enclosed room with wood floors and blue-padded walls, the space has been transformed into an open-air dirt field.

How's that possible?

Standing in the center is a tall figure wearing all black and a red flowing cape. He has a narrow face, angular cheekbones, and a pointy chin. His hair and beard are white, and his lips are curled into a strange smile. He's leaning on a black walking stick, his long fingers tapping impatiently on the silver cap. As we approach, I can't help but notice that his green eyes are focused only on me.

I have a bad feeling about this.

We fan out side-by-side, and no one says a word. Clearly, there aren't going to be any friendly introductions. Finally, Hexum breaks the silence.

"There is a rumor that we have a real vampire in our midst," he says, his raspy voice barely above a whisper. "Is that true?"

I peer at Rage who mouths, 'don't take the bait.'

"No answer?" Hexum continues, pacing back and forth. That's when I notice he walks with a pronounced limp, so I guess that walking stick isn't just for show.

"How disappointing," he continues. "I always thought vampires were kings of the monsters. Perhaps ours is more of a court jester."

Hang on. Did he just insult me? Then, I remember what Rage said, so I do my best to stay calm.

"I assume all of you know how rare it is to even glimpse a vampire in this day and age," Hexum says. "After all, vampires were thought to have been extinct, only existing in our nightmares. Yet, we supposedly have one right here in our presence. What an honor."

What is this guy's problem?

"The abilities of vampires are legendary," Hexum says, stopping suddenly in front of me and looking me dead in the eyes. "Are yours?"

Okay, this guy is getting under my skin.

"Here in Survival Skills," Hexum continues, "we will put your abilities to the test. We will see if you can live up to the standards of your ancestors. Shall we begin, Mr. Murray?"

I shoot a sideways glance at Rage and the others who are all staring at their feet. Clearly, no one is going to help me out here.

"I guess so," I say finally, my voice surprisingly soft.

"Ah, he speaks," Hexum says. "I was afraid you might be mute. Very well then, Mr. Murray, your first test is a simple one. Control the wolves."

Wolves? What wolves?

Suddenly, Hexum snaps his fingers and two gigantic, gray wolves appear out of nowhere across the way. Where'd they come from? The wild animals crouch low and start growling, looking at me like I'm their next meal.

"Ready, Mr. Murray?" Hexum says. "Go."

Um, what?

Just then, the wolves leap up and start chasing me.

So, I do what comes naturally. I take off.

"Stop it!" I hear Rage cry.

"Quiet!" Hexum barks. "I must see what he can do."

What I can do? All I can do is run for my life. I turn on the speed jets, putting as much distance between us as possible. But when I look over my shoulder, the wolves are still right on my tail. How is that possible?

"Cease!" Hexum commands.

Suddenly, the wolves vanish into thin air.

What's happening? And why am I still standing in the same spot? I mean, I must have run for miles.

"Strike one, Mr. Murray," Hexum says. "You failed to control the wolves. Now let us move to your next test. Free yourself from the glass container."

Did he say container?

Suddenly, a giant, glass tube drops from the sky, trapping me inside. I push against it, but it won't budge. I notice there's a small hole at the top, big enough for a mouse to squeeze through, but I can't reach it. And even if I could, I couldn't fit through it anyway.

Suddenly, my feet feel wet. I look down to find the tube filling with water! Where did that come from? The water is rising quickly, reaching the tops of my shoes, then my knees, then my waist.

Holy cow! If I don't get out of here, I'll drown!

I jump up to reach the hole, but it's too high!

"He's struggling!" Rage yells.

"Silence!" Hexum responds.

The water is up to my armpits! I'm going to drown in here! In front of everybody!

I close my eyes and scream.

"Stop!" Hexum commands.

Just like that, the water and the glass tube are gone.

And what's even weirder, my clothes are completely dry. It's like nothing happened.

"Strike two, Mr. Murray," Hexum says. "You have failed to escape from the glass container. Now for your third and final test. Fly."

Wait, what?

Suddenly, I'm standing on the edge of a high, rocky cliff. Where am I? I back away from the precipice and peer into the misty abyss. Great, it looks bottomless.

By now I know something bad is about to happen, I just don't know what.

Then, I hear an ear-piercing SHRILL behind me.

I duck just as a giant bat buzzes my head.

Gross!

The bat flaps off into the sky. Whew, that was close!

Suddenly, I hear more SHRILLS.

I turn slowly, only to find more bats heading my way.

Hundreds of them.

My heart starts pounding and I look for somewhere to hide, but there's no escape. The bats are coming so fast all I can do is shuffle back to the edge of the cliff.

My heel kicks a rock that tumbles over the edge.

I never hear it land.

I look back to find a nearly black sky. The bats are everywhere! My only option is to jump, but I can't!

There's no bottom!

Seconds later, they're on me. I kneel, blocking my face with my arms, but the creatures pummel me, pushing me backward. I try holding my ground, but I can't, and then…

I'm falling! I can't stop!

I'm going to die!

"Enough!" Hexum yells.

Just like that, the sensation of falling to my doom disappears, and I find myself lying on my back, my arms and legs spread out wide.

I'm alive! Thank goodness, I'm alive!

Then, I sense someone approaching.

"Strike three," Hexum says, with disappointment written all over his face.

"W-Why are you doing this?" I ask.

"Because my job is to sharpen your skills as a vampire," Hexum says. "The first test was to see if you could control wild animals. The second test was to see if you could turn your body into a mist and escape through a small opening. The third test was to see if you could transform into a bat and fly. These are the most basic abilities of a vampire. You, Mr. Murray, have none of them."

I look at the other kids who are just staring at me.

I feel so embarrassed.

"You may be a vampire by blood," he says, "but you are a rather limited vampire. If you wish to succeed in our line of work, you will need to push yourself harder than you have ever pushed yourself before. And if you don't, then you will die. And I don't think either of us wants that on our resumés, do we?"

But before I can answer he turns his back on me and claps sharply at the others. "This pathetic experiment is over. Students, take your places!"

CHAPTER NINE

STROLLING THROUGH THE GRAVEYARD

I don't think I could feel more useless if I tried.

The other kids attempt to cheer me up at dinner, but I'm not in the mood. In fact, I'm feeling so depressed I can't eat a thing. I try to smile and pretend everything is okay, but it's not.

According to Hexum, I'm a limited vampire. And what's worse is that I know he's right! I mean, how in the world am I supposed to battle the Dark Ones if I'm so pathetic? The short answer—I can't.

And the Monstrosities know it too.

I mean, they were forced to watch me make a total fool of myself. I'm pretty sure they won't be inviting me to join their team any time soon.

Some vampire I turned out to be.

As we head back to our rooms, I decide I'm going to run away once everyone has gone to sleep. I mean, why should I bother hanging around this joint? Plus, at this point, I'm pretty sure no one would miss me anyway.

Rage unlocks our door and flops onto his bed. As I head over to my side, I survey my things. I've never had so many clothes before. I could probably carry some of it, but the rest would only slow me down. I scoop a few pairs of clean underwear in my arms.

"You're taking this way too personally," Rage says.

"Taking what too personally?" I say, pretending not to know what he's talking about.

"Hexum's assessment," Rage says.

"How else am I supposed to take it?" I snap. "I failed every one of his tests. Every single one. Am I supposed to be happy about it?"

"It's your first day," Rage says. "Don't be so hard on yourself."

"Hexum called me 'limited,'" I say. "How'd you feel if he said that to you?"

"He has," Rage says. "Look, I failed all of my first tests too. And so did Stanphibian, and Hairball, and Aura. I warned you, you can't win with that guy."

"Hang on," I say. "Aura failed a test?"

"Yep," Rage says. "We all did. I told you, Hexum is a different kind of teacher. He pushes you hard. But he does it to make you better."

"He crossed the line," I say.

"Think so?" Rage says. "On my first day, I cried in front of the whole class. But look at me now. I'm still here, aren't I? I didn't quit. Will you?"

Darn it, he's on to me.

I never thought of myself as a quitter, but maybe I am. I mean, every time things get hard I take off. Hexum was tough on me, but is it really the end of the world?

I turn to find Rage looking at me earnestly, like a puppy wearing blue glasses. I drop the underwear.

"Okay, okay," I say. "I won't quit. I just don't get how he did all of those crazy tests. I mean, where did those wolves come from? And the creepy bats?"

"From your brain," Rage says, pointing to his head.

"What?"

"I told you," Rage says. "Hexum is a mentalist. He can tap into your brain and make you think that all of that stuff is really happening. We didn't see a wolf or a bat. Everything that happened was happening inside your own mind."

In my own mind? I'm so shocked I sit down. Is that why those wolves were right behind me even though I was running at top speed. And I guess that explains why my clothes were bone dry after the water test. Or why I didn't go splat after the bats knocked me off the cliff.

"I must have looked like a complete dweeb," I say.

"A total dweeb," Rage says. "But Hexum makes all of us look like dweebs now and then. He knows what buttons to push. He's a master at it. But if you stick with him, you'll get stronger."

"Yeah," I say. "I guess."

I'll need to get a whole lot stronger if I'm going to survive this nuthouse. I lay down on the bed and stare at the ceiling. I have that same itchy-feet-feeling I'd always get when living with a foster family got rough. But this time that feeling is being squashed by another one.

A feeling that I should stay.

I mean, I've never felt like I belonged anywhere before until I got here. I've never met kids like these.

Kids like me.

"By the way," Rage adds, "if you think Hexum is bad, you should have been here when that Faustius guy was around. Supposedly, he was a lunatic."

Faustius? Who's that? But then I remember seeing his name on that door with all the locks on it.

"How so?" I ask.

"Because he used to teach a subject called Black Magic," Rage says. "You know, evil incantations, curses, demon summoning. Stuff like that."

"Wow," I say. "That sounds hard core. What happened to him?"

"No one knows for sure," Rage says. "He was gone before I got here. But I heard he was more brutal than Hexum. Van Helsing has been looking for a replacement ever since."

I couldn't imagine anyone more brutal than Hexum.

Rage puts his arms behind his head and settles into his bed. He seems like a good kid, but I don't know much about him.

"So, what brought you here?" I ask.

Rage chuckles.

"What's so funny?" I ask.

"Nothing," he says. "It's just the way you phrased the question. I guess I literally *was* brought here. You see, I don't remember anything before the Van Helsing Academy."

"Seriously?" I ask.

"Yep," Rage says. "One day I opened my eyes, and I was lying in the infirmary with tubes sticking out all over the place. Van Helsing was there, with Crawler, and Dr. Hagella. They were telling me to stay calm, that everything was going to be okay. Of course, I was scared out of my mind. I remember the machines blaring and Crawler holding me down while they amped up the medicine. Eventually, I calmed down and they asked me a lot of questions, but I couldn't remember anything. I didn't even know my own name, let alone the names of my parents, or even my home address."

"Wow, is that still true?" I ask.

"Yep," he says. "Everything before here is gone. So, they enrolled me. They said this was the perfect place for a kid like me. Because of my powers, I got the code name Rage. And now here I am."

"I was going to ask about that," I say. "Does everybody get a code name?"

"Oh yeah," he says. "You'll get one eventually. But it has to relate to your abilities."

"So, why are you called Rage anyway?"

"Well..." Rage starts.

But just then, Aura phases through the door.

"Get up, people!" she orders. "Time to get moving! Monsters are on the prowl!"

"Aura, I told you to knock!" Rage complains. "I could have been naked!"

"Whatever," she says, rolling her eyes. "Get up, we've got a cemetery to visit. Hairball, InvisiBill, and Stanphibian are already downstairs."

"Um, sorry, but what's going on here?" I ask.

"There's another grave robbery in progress," she says. "This is the third one in the last two weeks. This time we can catch the thieves red-handed."

"And how do you know that?" I ask.

"I'm a ghost, remember? I'm wired into the spirit network."

"Gotcha," I say.

"Okay, okay," Rage says, hopping off his bed and pulling on his sweatshirt. "How far away is it?"

"We're in luck," she says. "This one is only a few towns over. Hurry up. Hairball's driving."

"Hang on," I say. "I thought we weren't supposed to be running around at night, especially off campus. What about Vi Clops? You know, that scary gigantic mountain-of-a-woman with the enormous eyeball. Remember her?"

I certainly did. She pretty much told me she'd swallow me whole if she caught me wandering around after curfew.

"Seriously?" Aura says, arms crossed.

"Um, yeah," I say.

"Okay, then you stay here," she says. She turns to leave, then stops and throws me an icy stare. "Maybe Hexum was right about you."

Then, she phases through the door.

Seconds later, Rage is right behind her. He opens the door, shrugs his shoulders, and leaves.

I'm all alone.

Great.

I'm sure Aura thinks I'm a total loser. First, I looked like a complete dork in Hexum's class, and now I'm just lying here while the rest of the Monstrosities try to stop a grave robbery.

My chances of making the team just keep shrinking. I stare at Rage's empty bed. Then, I remember what Aura said: *Maybe Hexum was right about you.*

Darn it!

I grab my hoodie and bolt out the door.

***

Thankfully, the kids are still in the lobby. I catch Aura half-smiling when I show up, but she quickly wipes it from her face.

"Sorry," I whisper. "I'm a bonehead, okay?"

"Apology accepted," she whispers back. "And yes, you are."

"Why didn't you leave yet?" I ask.

"We were about to," she says. "But we can't find InvisiBill. Feel free to help us look around."

While the team searches for InvisiBill, I'm sweating bullets. In my mind's eye, I see Vi Clops rounding the corner, her angry red eye heading straight for me. I guess Aura senses my nervousness because she just shakes her head and points towards the Administration Office.

Just then, I hear a SAWING noise coming from the partially open door. I tiptoe over and peek inside. To my surprise, Vi Clops is lying face down on the counter, snoring like a busted vacuum cleaner. Next to her are a dozen empty pizza boxes.

"She'll sleep for hours," Aura says, scaring me out of my skin. "A cyclops always falls asleep after a big meal. It pays to know your Monsterology."

"Right," I whisper. "Good tip."

A few minutes later, Rage accidentally sits on InvisiBill, who was napping on one of the couches. Mystery solved, but boy did Aura rip into him.

After that, we leave the lobby and dash through a series of corridors. It feels like we're running through an endless maze, but the Monstrosities seem to know exactly where they're going, so I'm thinking they've done this before. Like, lots of times before.

Finally, we reach a solid stone wall and I think we've hit a dead end. But then Hairball pulls down a sconce, and the whole wall slides open, revealing a narrow hallway. Well, I wasn't expecting that.

We squeeze through one by one, and the next thing I know, we pop out the back of Monster House and onto the school grounds. We dart across the grass beneath a full moon and head towards a big building I've never seen before.

"Where are we going?" I yell out to Rage as my heart pumps a million miles a second.

"The garage," Rage whispers back.

The garage? That's the biggest garage I've ever seen in my life. We run through the open hangar door to find dozens of parked vehicles, like buses, jeeps, and Crawler's motorcycle. I run my hand along Crawler's sidecar. Seeing it again reminds me of just how freaked out I was when I first got here.

If only Crawler could see me now.

Aura tells us to keep watch as Hairball hotwires a nearby jeep. Rage and I take the hangar door.

"You sure this is a good idea?" I whisper.

"Probably not," Rage whispers back.

"Does Hairball have a driver's license?" I ask.

"Dude, don't let the facial hair fool you. The kid's only twelve-years-old."

"Oh," I whisper. "Wonderful."

Suddenly, the engine ROARS and we pile inside. I'm squished in the backseat between Stanphibian, who smells like an aquarium, and InvisiBill, who just plain smells.

The next thing I know, we're swerving down the driveway towards the front gate. I remember Crawler getting eye-scanned to open the campus gate, so I'm pretty sure this will be a short joyride. We pull up to the security booth, and right on cue, the eye-scanning device extends towards the car.

Well, I can finally breathe.

This should put an end to this little adventure.

But to my surprise, Aura crosses over to the driver's side and sticks her hand right through the scanner! Electric blue currents shoot across the face of the device and then there's a loud POPPING noise.

Suddenly, the front gate slides open.

She short-circuited the machine!

"Gun it!" Aura orders.

Hairball pounds the gas and we're off like a rocket!

As we drive away, I look back to see the campus getting smaller behind us, and I'm pretty sure Van Helsing wouldn't approve of what we're doing.

***

After a perilous drive going way over the speed limit, we finally arrive at the cemetery. Somehow, and I still don't know how, I manage not to toss my cookies.

Hairball rolls up to the iron-wrought front gate.

No surprise, it's locked.

A dense fog hugs the ground, adding an extra creepy dimension no one needs right now. Behind the gate, I can make out tombstones organized in neat little rows, but there's no sign of any grave robbers.

"What now?" Hairball asks.

"Now we go inside, fur brain," Aura says. "We won't stop any grave robbers sitting out here."

"Got it," Hairball says, slamming on the gas.

Before I can object, the jeep SMASHES through the gates, and I see InvisiBill's window go down. The next thing I know, I hear InvisiBill retching.

Great, invisi-barf.

Hairball flies through the cemetery with Aura shouting directions. The fog is so thick you can't see more than a foot in front of the jeep, and the two of them are arguing like crazy over which way to go.

Between Hairball's horrible driving and the stench coming from InvisiBill, I'm starting to feel nauseous myself. I'm about to tell Hairball to slow down when our headlights suddenly flash over a group of figures standing waste deep in a grave.

"Stop!" Aura yells. "Right there! Those people are the grave robbers!"

"Um," Hairball says, "Those aren't people."

"I-Is that …?" Rage stammers.

"Zombies?" Hairball says. "Yeah."

I look out the windshield and my stomach drops to my toes. Four hideous creatures stare back with red, unblinking eyes. They're disheveled looking, with wild hair, ripped clothes, and huge chunks of skin missing from their faces.

"I'm gonna puke," InvisiBill says. "Again."

No one moves. It's like each group is shocked to see the other. That's when I notice three of the zombies are males and one is a female. For a minute, they almost look like store mannequins at a Halloween costume shop. Then, out of the blue, the males start coming out of the grave, walking towards us in a slow, herky-jerky manner!

"Get us out of here!" Rage yells.

Hairball throws the jeep into reverse, and then lurches forward, SLAMMING into a tree!

My head smashes into Stanphibian's fishbowl and everything becomes a jumbled blur. For a second, all I see are stars. Then, I realize the jeep isn't moving.

Hairball turns the key and the jeep SPUTTERS.

"It won't start!" Hairball yells.

There's smoke coming from the hood.

"Monstrosities, move out!" Aura commands.

No one needs a second invitation. We jump out of the vehicle and scatter. Given my lack of fighting skills, I stick close to Hairball because he's the largest.

"Don't let them bite you!" I hear Rage yell.

The zombies spread out. One of them, wearing a suit and tie, approaches Hairball and me, arms outstretched. He smells putrid, like rotten meat. I'm about to bolt when I realize Hairball is standing his ground.

"Um, Hairball?" I say. "Shouldn't you—"

But before I can finish my sentence, Hairball rears back his giant fist and punches the zombie into the next zip code!

"Holy cow!" I say.

The other Monstrosities are equally as impressive. Aura and Stanphibian team up against a zombie to my left. I watch Aura bait it, but when the creature lunges it passes right through her. Then, Stanphibian takes over, spearing it with a giant branch. He spins around at incredible speed and then lets the branch go, launching the zombie high into a tree.

On the other side, I see the last zombie dude turning aimlessly in circles. Knowing InvisiBill, he's probably tapping it on the shoulder and running to the other side. But his fun and games are about to end as Hairball heads over to help.

Then, I realize I haven't seen Rage.

Where is he?

Suddenly, I remember there's one zombie left—the female! She was still in the grave, but when I look over, I can't see anything through the fog.

Then, a terrible thought crosses my mind.

What if she's got Rage?

Without thinking, I take off for the grave. When I arrive the zombie isn't there, but neither is Rage. I look into the grave itself and notice the coffin is busted open.

It's empty inside!

That zombie stole all of the bones!

I glance up at the tombstone, which reads:

DR. EUGENE ALBERT
INVENTOR, PHILOSOPHER,
PHILANTHROPIST

Something moves behind a cluster of trees.

Is that the zombie? And does she have Rage?

I can't let her escape, but the other kids are too far away to help. I've got no choice.

I turn on my super speed and break for the woods, but the fog is so thick I can barely see where I'm going. I reach the area where I thought I saw the movement, but there's no sign of the zombie or Rage. I don't know what to do. I'm not trained to fight a zombie by myself, and I can't see the other kids. I could head back, but I'd risk losing the trail—and quite possibly Rage—for good.

There's only one choice.

I figure I can cover the woods quicker with my speed, but as soon as I power up, I feel myself powering down. What's going on? Then, I remember I was so upset about Hexum that I didn't eat dinner.

Genius move.

I could yell for help, but that'll just tell the zombie where to come eat me. Out of the corner of my eye, I spot a branch lying on the ground. It's long and sharp and looks like it can do some serious damage, so I pick it up and keep moving.

It's quiet. Eerily quiet.

The only sounds I hear are my feet crunching

through the leaves and the beating of my own heart. After a few minutes of aimless walking, I realize I've lost the trail.

There's no point in being subtle now.

"Rage!" I call out. "Rage, where are you?"

But there's no answer.

I take a few more steps.

Suddenly, I hear a CRACK behind me.

"Rage?"

I turn, hoping to see my friend, but instead, I see something far worse.

It's… a werewolf!

Seriously? Now?

The beast lets out an ear-piercing HOWL.

And five more pop up behind him.

MONSTEROLOGY 101 FIELD GUIDE

ZOMBIE

CLASSIFICATION:

Type: Undead
Sub-Type: Not applicable
Height: Variable
Weight: Variable
Eye Color: Red
Hair Color: Variable

KNOWN ABILITIES:

- Superhuman Strength
- Travels in packs
- Pursues victims relentlessly
- May bite victims, turning them into fellow Zombies

KNOWN WEAKNESSES:

- Low intelligence
- Vulnerable to fire
- Extremely slow with poor reflexes
- Brittle body can be easily destroyed

DANGER LEVEL:

MEDIUM ▪▪□□

TIPS TO AVOID AN UNWANTED ENCOUNTER:

- Avoid cramped spaces
- Don't stand in front of windows
- Stay alert for large, slow-moving crowds
- Travel only during the daytime

CHAPTER TEN

SERIOUSLY NOT AGAIN

I've decided I really, really hate werewolves.

Not only do they eat people, but they also have a terrible habit of showing up at the worst possible times.

Like now, for instance.

With six of the hairy monsters surrounding me, I need to hit the pause button on my search for Rage and put all of my attention on the task at hand—staying alive!

I spin around, jabbing with my spear to keep the beasts at bay when I notice for the first time that werewolves come in all shapes and sizes. Some are tall and skinny, while others are short and stout. Three have brown fur, while two are red, and one is black. Then, it dawns on me that now probably isn't the best time to be making useless observations like this. I guess the mind works in funny ways when one is facing impending death.

As the creatures form a circle of teeth and claws around me, my heart is pounding out of my chest. I mean, all I have to defend myself is a stick! I hold it up high, ready to thrust at a moment's notice, but there's no way I can hold off one werewolf, let alone six!

The last time this happened I was miraculously saved by Crawler. But this time I'm not expecting miracles to strike twice. Then, I remember Hexum's class.

If I can turn myself into a bat, or a cloud of mist, then I could sail out of here scot-free!

But how the heck do I do that?

I mean, Hexum only told me it's possible for vampires other than me. But he didn't tell me how I can do it for myself.

Just then, the black werewolf grunts and they all take a step closer, tightening the ring around me. Now I barely have room to operate! They're standing just outside of my reach, but close enough that I can smell their stench—and boy do they need breath mints!

I sweep my spear, but they barely react, which tells me they're less than intimidated. If I don't do something—anything—fast, I'm dead meat.

Am I overthinking this vampire thing?

Maybe I just need to go for it.

"Be a bat, be a bat, be a bat," I chant quickly, but nothing happens! No wings. No tiny feet. No air time.

I'm still a kid.

Let's try the mist thing.

"Be a mist, be a mist, be a mist."

But no luck either.

Then, I remember Hexum's first test, controlling wolves! I pick out the black-furred one and send Jedi mind tricks its way.

Go home. Please, go home.

But it just narrows its eyes and lets out a ferocious growl. Okay, Hexum is right, I really suck at this whole vampire thing. Time for plan B—total panic!

"Help!" I yell. "Aura! Hairball! Stanphibian! Even InvisiBill! If you're out there, help!"

Unfortunately, no cavalry comes to the rescue, and I'm not surprised. I've probably drifted miles away from the cemetery and way out of earshot. The Monstrosities are either searching for me, or they figured I'm already zombie food by now and split.

A string of drool falls from the black-furred one's mouth, and then it bares its sharp teeth and SNARLS.

This is it!

I close my eyes, waiting for the end.

ROOOOAAARRRRRR!

Um, what's that?

That didn't sound like any werewolf.

Suddenly, there's a series of high-pitched YELPS, and when I open my eyes, I see werewolves scattering all over the place.

What's happening?

THUD!

The ground buckles, knocking me on my rear.

Was that… an earthquake?

THUD!

I bounce like a kernel in a popcorn popper.

Then, there's a loud SNAP, and I realize that's no earthquake. Something is heading our way.

Something big.

My instincts tell me to run, but I stay put. For some crazy reason, I feel like I need to see what's about to happen next. And apparently, the werewolves feel the same way, because instead of fleeing, they're huddling up, preparing themselves for whatever is coming.

Then, the footsteps stop.

The werewolves sniff the air and shoot each other nervous looks.

It's super quiet. Why's it so darn—

BOOM!

I crabwalk backward as two gigantic trees come toppling to the ground like twigs, nearly crushing the werewolves. I get back on my feet, and when I look over at the brush, out steps the biggest, baddest, most horrific monster I've seen yet!

I pick up my jaw and try to take it all in. It must be ten feet tall, with curly, blond hair, purple skin, and an unfriendly scowl. Its body is inexplicably humungous, with boulder-sized muscles bulging from its arms and legs. And strangely, its clothes are shredded across its broad chest and thick thighs.

With a thundering step, the giant strides into the center and glares at me. My legs turn to jelly and I seriously consider asking the werewolves to adopt me.

But then I notice the glasses.

There's a pair of blue glasses wrapped tightly around its neck by a cord. And if I didn't know better, I'd say they looked like... Rage's glasses?

Suddenly, two werewolves jump on the monster's back and begin clawing at his skin. The behemoth lets out a tremendous ROAR and reaches back, grabbing the werewolves by the scruffs of their necks and tossing them into the trees so hard the trunks splinter.

The werewolves crumble to the ground.

Neither gets back up.

Seconds later, the four remaining werewolves approach at once, two from the front and two from the back. The monolith holds its ground, watching them closely. It's like they're playing a game of chicken, waiting to see who will make the first move.

Then, the red werewolf charges from the front. With shocking speed, the purple giant steps aside and grabs him from behind. The others jump in, but the brute uses the red werewolf like a baseball bat, clobbering the others into the air and out of sight. When he's done, he chucks the red werewolf into the night sky.

Well, so much for the werewolves.

Now it's just us!

I put my hands in the air.

"Rage?" I say. "Is that you? It's me, Bram."

It steps towards me with a curious expression, and as I look into its blue eyes, I realize that this monster is, in fact, my friend Rage.

"Rage?" I ask. "Are you hurt?"

But he doesn't answer. He just stares at me.

"Rage? Remember me? I'm your roommate."

His brow furrows, and he ROARS, blowing my hair straight back.

"Um, you do remember me, don't you?"

The creature raises his massive fists.

He's gonna pound me!

Suddenly, I hear a THWIP and feel something buzz by my ear. The next thing I know, Rage CRIES out so loud the trees shake. And when I look up, I see a large dart sticking out of his arm.

Rage looks at me with an odd expression.

"Get out of the way!" comes a familiar voice.

Something grabs me from behind right before the giant comes crashing down, smashing face-first into the ground.

I breathe a sigh of relief. There's no doubt that if I were still standing there, I'd be a kid pancake.

"Just in time," Crawler says.

The man-spider is holding a huge smoking gun the size of a bazooka. I look back at the monster, but he's gone! And in his place is a small, blond-haired boy.

Rage!

But he's not moving.

"D-Did you...?" I stammer.

"No," Crawler says. "I used a tranquilizer strong enough to knock out a herd of elephants. He'll be okay, but he'll be out for a while."

"I-I can't believe that was him," I say. "Now I know why he's called Rage. I thought he was going to kill me."

"He might have," Crawler says. "He has no control of his emotions when he's in that state. He's dangerous. But that's just one reason you kids shouldn't be sneaking around alone at night. Those werewolves are another."

"Yeah," I say. "I seem to have a thing with werewolves. Maybe I need to change my brand of deodorant."

"Werewolves have an incredible sense of smell," Crawler says. "They know your scent by now."

Then, I have a weird thought. "So, if they know my smell, how come they haven't tracked me down at school yet?"

"The Van Helsing Academy is protected by Supernatural artifacts that shield it from evil," Crawler says, slinging the gun over his shoulder. "When you're on campus, you're safe. But once you exit those gates, all bets are off. Remember that, because Van Helsing may not send me to rescue you next time."

"I will," I say. "Wait, Van Helsing sent you?"

"Yep," Crawler says, scooping up Rage. "Up until about an hour ago, I was enjoying a pretty relaxing night. So, I think you owe me one. Now tell me, what exactly were you kids doing out here?"

"Um, well, we—"

"—were just looking for a late-night snack," comes

Aura's voice.

I turn to find the Monstrosities walking towards us.

I can't even tell you how happy I am to see them!

"You know how it is, Crawler," Aura says. "We were studying late for one of Professor Seward's pop quizzes and got a little hungry. We just took a wrong turn on our way to a fast food joint. Isn't that right, Bram?"

Aura shoots me a serious look. That's a cold, hard lie. But if I don't back her up, she'll never trust me again.

"Um, yeah," I say, swallowing hard. "That's it in a nutshell."

"Is that so?" Crawler says, eyeing me warily. "Seems like a shaky story coming from a ghost who doesn't eat. So, which one of you jokers is responsible for damaging the jeep?"

"Jeep?" Hairball says, his voice cracking. "What jeep?"

"That one," Crawler says.

Just then, the jeep comes rolling towards us. The hood is popped open, the windshield is smashed, and the bumper is hanging halfway off the front. It looks so badly damaged I don't know how it's running at all, until I realize it's not being driven, it's being carried—by a gazillion spiders!

"Uh oh," Hairball says.

"I hope you've got car insurance, Hairball," Crawler says. "Because I can't wait for Van Helsing to see this one."

Ten

***

The other kids get to see Van Helsing as a group, but I'm not so lucky. Instead, Crawler instructs me to wait outside until Van Helsing is finished with them. I don't know what's worse, getting the punishment, or being forced to think about getting the punishment.

An hour later, the door finally opens, and my friends file out with their heads down. Strangely, no one says a word so it must have been pretty bad. Aura doesn't even look my way.

The only one spared is Rage, who is recovering in the infirmary. Dr. Hagella thinks he'll be okay, but only time will tell. He still hasn't woken up yet.

I watch as the Monstrosities walk away, except for InvisiBill, who I can't see at all. Then, they round the corner and disappear from view.

It's my turn.

I know I need to go inside and face the music, but for some reason, my eyes are fixated on Professor Faustius' door across the way. I study the 'Entry Forbidden' sign hanging from his doorknob and wonder what happened to that guy. Rage told me he used to teach Black Magic, so maybe he summoned a demon who gobbled him up or something?

Well, whatever it is, I'm sure it's not good.

Okay, I figure I've stalled long enough.

I take a deep breath and enter Van Helsing's office.

It's just as warm as I remembered, with piles of junk precariously balanced upon other piles of junk. How he finds anything in this place is a mystery to me. I carefully pick my way through the clutter, nearly making it through unscathed until I step on something that SQUEAKS and scampers away, nearly giving me a heart attack!

Once I regain my composure, I pause before turning the final corner because I know what's waiting for me on the other side. Then, I step out to meet my fate.

Van Helsing is sitting in his chair, feeding logs into the fire. He's as heavily dressed as before, complete with a sweater, scarf, and gloves. The flames from the fire cast dancing shadows on his furrowed brow. His blue eyes meet mine, but he doesn't say anything, so I take a seat across from him and await my sentencing.

It's so unbearably warm that sweat starts dripping from my forehead. I wait for Van Helsing to start talking but he simply stares at me. In the meantime, a hundred horrible scenarios unfold in my head, each more terrible than the one before.

Is he going to tell me he's disappointed in me? Is he going to throw me in a dungeon? Is he going to expel me from the academy?

Suddenly, he breaks the silence.

"What should your punishment be?" he asks.

My eyebrows go sky high. Um, what? Did he just ask me what my own punishment should be? Was he serious?

I mean, no one has ever asked me to pick my own punishment before. I must have misheard him.

"I-I'm sorry," I stammer. "Did you say you wanted me to decide my own punishment?"

"Yes," he says. "At the Van Helsing Academy, students are accountable for their behavior and misbehavior. Therefore, it falls on you to pick your punishment. I only ask that you weigh the transgression and pick the most reasonable punishment."

Wow, that's amazing!

My mind fills with possibilities.

Maybe a day of television? Or no homework for a week? Or maybe all of the Swedish Fish I can eat?

But when I look at Van Helsing, I know those aren't punishments at all. He's expecting me to be responsible—to find a punishment that fits the crime.

So, let's see. We snuck off campus, wrecked his jeep, and put all of our lives in danger, including Crawler's life.

What punishment is worthy of all of that?

Suddenly, the worst thing possible pops into my head.

"An extra session with Professor Hexum?" I blurt out unexpectedly. "Just him and me."

I regret it as soon as I say it.

This time Van Helsing raises his eyebrows. "That is a fair punishment. Your session will be scheduled for tomorrow afternoon. Thank you for being accountable for your actions. You are now dismissed."

Really? That's it? I'm so shocked I sit there dumbfounded for a minute before standing up.

Then, a curious thought springs to mind.

"Headmaster, can I ask you something?"

"Yes, Bram."

"What happened to Professor Faustius?"

Van Helsing's left eyebrow raises for a second, and he says—

"Professor Faustius is no longer employed here."

But before I can follow up, he turns away and looks into the fire.

It's clear he doesn't want to talk about it.

So, I take the hint and leave.

VAN HELSING ACADEMY

STUDENT ASSESSMENT

VITALS:
NAME: Unknown
EYES: Blue
HAIR: Blond
HEIGHT: 4'4"/10'3"
WEIGHT: 72/615 lbs

NOTES: Kind and docile in human form. Transforms into angry, uncontrollable beast with extraordinary strength. Has no memory of transformation.

CODENAME: RAGE

CLASSIFICATION TYPE:
Abnormal — Jekyll/Hyde

SUPERNATURAL ASSESSMENT:

STRENGTH	●●●●●
AGILITY	●●○○○
FIGHTING	●●●○○
INTELLECT	●○○○○
CONTROL	●○○○○

TEACHABLE?	Yes	No
VAN HELSING	●	○
CRAWLER	●	○
HOLMWOOD	○	●
SEWARD	○	●
MORRIS	●	○
HEXUM	○	●
~~FAUSTIUS~~	~~○~~	~~○~~

RISK LEVEL: HIGH

CHAPTER ELEVEN

BAT-TERED AND BRUISED

It's the wee hours of the morning and we're all in the infirmary checking up on Rage. Dr. Hagella said he's stabilized, which is great news, but he's been sound asleep for at least four hours. He has way more color in his cheeks than the last time I saw him—which thankfully isn't purple.

No one is feeling particularly chatty. After our discussions with Van Helsing, we're all lost in our thoughts. Not surprisingly, I can't seem to get my upcoming punishment with Hexum out of my mind. I'm kicking myself for not coming up with something—and I mean anything—else.

After a while, Stanphibian, Hairball, and InvisiBill head back to Monster House for some shuteye. Aura isn't ready to go back yet, so I decide to keep her company.

The two of us sit in silence as Rage snores like a baby hog. I want to say something to break the noticeable tension in the air, but she doesn't seem so interested in talking to me.

Finally, I can't take it anymore.

"Are you mad at me or something?" I ask.

"Mad?" she says. "Why would I be mad at you?"

"I don't know," I say. "You've been awfully quiet since you left Van Helsing's office."

"Don't be ridiculous," she says. "I'm not mad at you. I'm mad at myself. This whole mess was my fault. I'm the one who found out about the grave robbers. I'm the one who forced everyone to go. I'm the one responsible for Rage getting hurt."

"Don't be so hard on yourself," I say. "You didn't know that would happen."

"But it was my responsibility," she says. "I knew going to the cemetery would be risky, and I should have made sure we were better prepared. But I didn't, and Rage nearly got killed. Anyway, I let Van Helsing know that I'm the one to blame, so I should face all of the consequences."

"What did he say about that?" I ask.

"He thanked me for my honesty," she says. "But he still made everyone come up with their own punishments. He said none of them had to follow me. He said they were responsible for making their own decisions."

She pauses, clearly upset.

"I'm sorry I asked you to lie to Crawler," she adds. "That wasn't right either."

"That's okay," I say. "But to Van Helsing's point, I guess I could've decided not to do it. But I still don't understand why you wanted me to lie to Crawler in the first place?"

"I don't know," she says. "I guess I thought we could handle it. I mean, if we could solve the mystery, we could show Van Helsing how capable we are."

"I think everyone knows how capable you are," I say. "You're the smartest person in our class. Like, it's not even close."

"Thanks," she says, brushing a strand of hair from her forehead. "But I don't feel very capable. I mean, look at me, I'm a freaking ghost. I'm here, but I'm not. I used to love to dance and act. Now I'll never be able to do those things again. I go crazy thinking about all the things I'll miss out on. Like driving a car, or going to prom, or my first kiss—"

She stops and shoots me an embarrassed look.

If I weren't so pale, I'm sure I'd be beet red.

"It… it must be tough," I manage to say.

"Yeah, it stinks," she says.

She looks depressed, so I figure I should try changing the subject. "So, about that mystery. Why do you think those zombies wanted those bones anyway?"

"I've been trying to figure that out," she says, her eyes widening with excitement. "Like, is there a pattern? The first grave they hit was of a man named Jonah Covington. I did some research on him. He was an Olympic gold medalist in the late nineteenth century who is still considered to be the greatest athlete of all time. He was supposed to be really tall and strong. He set all kinds of records."

"Really?" I say. "I didn't know about that one."

"Yeah," she says. "And the second grave belonged to a military corporal named Lloyd McAdams. He was a sharpshooter during World War I and was known as the best shot of the twentieth century."

"Totally weird," I say. I remember seeing the newspaper headline for that one back at the New England Home for Troubled Boys.

"Very weird," she says. "But it gets weirder. Tonight, they stole the bones of Dr. Eugene Albert. He was a brilliant scientist who won the Nobel Prize for his work in physics and quantum mechanics."

"What would a bunch of zombies want with the bones of an athlete, a sharpshooter, and a brainiac?" I ask. "I thought they only cared about eating flesh."

"Exactly," she says. "I've been wondering the same thing. But then I realized the zombies probably didn't want the bones for themselves. They must be working for someone else."

"Like who?"

"Like the Dark Ones," she says matter-of-factly.

A chill runs down my spine. The Dark Ones? Could they be behind this? And what about those werewolves? Van Helsing told me they worked for the Dark Ones too. Clearly, they're still after me.

Suddenly, Dr. Hagella pops in. "You both should go

to bed. Rage needs his rest, and so do you. Goodnight."

"Okay, Doc," Aura says. "You know I can't sleep, but I get it. Goodnight."

As we head out, the sun is climbing over the horizon. I can probably get in a shower before breakfast, but there's no way I'll be getting any rest. Today is going to be a busy day.

Especially with Hexum.

"Just out of curiosity," I say, "what did you pick for your punishment?"

"I told Van Helsing I'd alphabetize his private library for him," she says, rolling her eyes. "You've seen the state of his office, right? Trust me, his library is much, much worse."

"I can't even imagine," I say. "But how can you do that? I mean, you're a ghost. Sorry."

"No, it's okay," she says. "Hexum has been teaching me how to use my own 'aura' to control the molecules around me and move objects around. He calls it 'telekinesis.' I'm still learning how to do it. It takes a lot of concentration, but that's how I keep my Monstrosities badge on."

"Really?" I say, noticing for the first time that her silver badge isn't pinned to her sweater, but floating in front of her body. "Wow. That's cool."

"Thanks," she says. "I'm no pro yet, but I figure I can handle moving some books around. It'll be good practice anyway. And since I don't need sleep, I figure I can tackle it over a few nights. How about you? What punishment did you pick?"

"A one-on-one with Hexum," I say sheepishly.

"Seriously?" she says. "Boy, you must really feel guilty about what we did."

"Either that," I say, "or I'm a big dope."

"No comment," she says.

"Gee, thanks," I say.

Our eyes meet, and we laugh.

***

I'm pretty much a train wreck all day. All I can think about is my dreaded appointment with Hexum, which pretty much makes me a space cadet in all of my other classes.

In Monsterology, Professor Holmwood makes me write 'I will pay attention in class' one hundred times on the chalkboard after I fail to respond to her questions. In Supernatural History, I struggle through Professor Seward's pop quiz on monsters in the medieval era. And in Paranormal Science, I manage to temporarily blind myself with a flash bomb.

It's hard to imagine things getting worse.

But then comes Survival Skills.

No sooner had we lined up, when—

"Attention!" Hexum commands. "Today's class is canceled. I expect all of you to practice your exercises on your own."

What? Really?

This is incredible news!

"Except for you, Mr. Murray," Hexum says. "Today, you and I will be having a private, double session."

Wait, what?

A double session? That's totally unfair! I told Van Helsing I'd have one extra session for my punishment, not two. This is injustice! This is criminal!

"The rest of you are dismissed," Hexum says.

As I jealously watch the others walk away, I catch Hairball snickering. Oh, when I get my hands on that giant, flea-bitten rug…

But then I see Aura.

She mouths 'good luck,' and then floats away.

Luck? I suspect I'll need more than luck if I'm going to survive this. The door SLAMS shut behind the last kid, echoing through the chamber.

Great, my worst nightmare has come true.

I'm alone with Hexum.

For two flippin' hours.

My back tightens up.

Hexum paces back and forth like some kind of a predator, which I guess makes me his prey. But I'm not opening my mouth. The more time he wastes doing this, the less time I'll have to interact with him.

Then, he wheels on me.

Uh-oh.

"Mr. Murray," he says, "I suspect you do not like me. Would I be correct in this assumption?"

I'm stunned. Of course he's correct, but am I supposed to tell him that? This feels like a trap. If I tell him the truth, I'll lose. But if I lie, somehow I'll lose again. But maybe bigger.

"Mr. Murray, I asked you a direct question. It would be polite to provide an answer."

What should I do? I have no choice but to go for it.

"You're correct," I say firmly. "I don't like you."

"Thank you," he says, raising an eyebrow. "I respect your brutal honesty, and I certainly understand if you left our last meeting feeling frustrated. No doubt it was a difficult day for you. But I am afraid your difficulty is just beginning. You see, Mr. Murray, my job is not to like you or dislike you. My job is to teach you how to get the most out of your abilities so you do not die. Do you understand, Mr. Murray?"

Strangely, I do.

I nod.

"Excellent," he says. "So, our first encounter was difficult out of necessity. After all, we needed to understand where the bar was set. Do you agree?"

I nod again.

"Excellent," he says. "I am glad you agree. Unfortunately, what we learned is that the bar is set so low, I am doubtful we will be able to raise it."

Speaking of low, that's pretty much how I'm feeling.

"But it is my job to try, Mr. Murray. So that is precisely what I will do. Now, perhaps we should start with something a bit more elementary this time. Do you know our motto here at the Van Helsing Academy?"

His question catches me off guard. Motto? What's that? But then I remember the black banner and the saying beneath the Van Helsing crest.

"You must believe in things you cannot imagine."

"Very good, Mr. Murray. Yes, that is correct. You must believe in things you cannot imagine. Do you know what that means?"

He's got me there. I've never really thought about it.

"I suppose it means there's more to this world than meets the eye," I say.

"In part," Hexum says, his lips curling into a thin smile. "It means there are things in this world that cannot be explained by science. You see, Mr. Murray, there are two types of creatures in this world, and they live by entirely different sets of rules. There are the Naturals, ordinary creatures, living their pedestrian lives according to the laws of nature. You know them well. They go to school, they go to work, they have offspring, they die."

Well, that makes being human sound lovely.

"But there is another type of creature," he continues. "The Supernatural creature, who lives by a force far more chaotic and unpredictable than nature. A force so powerful it can give life back to the dead. Tell me, Mr. Murray, which set of rules do you live by?"

"The Supernatural one?" I say.

"Very good," Hexum says. "You are a Supernatural, after all. But you do not think like a Supernatural. No, no. You think like a Natural. And when you think like a Natural, it is hard to 'believe in things you cannot imagine.' Do you understand, Mr. Murray?"

"I-I think so."

"If you are truly going to be a Supernatural, you must learn to think like a Supernatural. This will be the focus of our lesson today."

Suddenly, a lightbulb flashes in my head. Maybe that's why this vampire thing isn't working. Maybe it's because I'm not thinking like a vampire. I'm thinking like a normal kid—a Natural—but I'm not.

"Enough talk," Hexum continues, "now we begin."

Hexum taps his walking stick on the floor, and I realize my pain is about to begin.

***

At dinner, I can barely lift my fork to my face.

And it's not just because my arm is sore, which it is, but also because I don't have an ounce of brainpower left. After an afternoon with Hexum, I'm mentally fried.

"You okay?" Hairball asks. "You look like a zombie."

"I'm not sure," I murmur. "I just experienced the worst two hours of my entire life."

"What did he make you do?" Aura asks. As usual, she's not eating anything.

"Turn into a bat," I say.

"How'd that go?" InvisiBill asks. I can't see him, but a slice of pizza magically lifts off of his tray.

"Not well," I say. "Over and over and over again."

"I'm so sorry, Bram," Aura says.

"I think Hexum is convinced I'm a complete waste of vampire DNA."

"Ouch," Stanphibian says.

Well, if I didn't know how bad it was, I know it now because Stanphibian rarely says anything. But is it my fault I can't turn into a bat? Maybe not all vampires are meant to be bats. Maybe I'm just not your typical vampire. I mean, look at me now. It's not like I'm sitting here sucking blood for dinner.

"Hey, gang!" comes a familiar voice.

"Rage!" we all exclaim.

"It's great to be back," he says, sliding his tray onto the table and squeezing in between Stanphibian and Hairball.

"How do you feel?" I ask.

"Great!" he says, stabbing into his steak with his fork. "Better than great actually. I needed that rest."

We watch him stuff his face like he hasn't eaten in days. He seems completely normal. Nothing like the purple beast that nearly squished me to death.

"Just out of curiosity, do you remember anything

that happened?" I ask.

"Nope," he says, looking at me with a screwy expression on his face. "The last thing I remember is that female zombie taking a swing at me. After that, nothing."

Wow. Okay then.

"Well, we're glad you're back," Aura says. "You scared us for a while."

"A long while," Hairball says.

"Dr. Hagella wants me to sit out of Survival Skills for a few weeks," Rage says. "She put this thing on me to monitor my blood pressure."

He raises his right arm to show us a device wrapped around his wrist with big, flashing numbers on it.

"Well, your blood pressure looks normal," Aura says.

"Thank goodness," I say, "for everyone's sake."

We all laugh, including Rage.

"So, I also have some exciting news," Aura says. "While Bram was being tortured by Hexum, I used my free time to start cataloging Van Helsing's private library. You'll never guess what I found."

"Van Helsing's sense of humor?" Hairball says.

"No," she says. "A copy of The Alchemy of Reanimation, Volume I."

"Reani-what?" Rage asks, his mouth full.

"Reanimation," Aura says. "It's the science of bringing the dead back to life."

Suddenly, I remember my conversation with Hexum. It sounds like some Natural was using science to bend the laws of nature, which probably isn't a good thing.

"It's a pretty fascinating read," she says. "It has all of this theory on how to do it, with charts and calculations and stuff. But to do it, you need the skeleton of a dead person."

"So?" InvisiBill says as we're forced to watch his chewed pizza rolling down his throat.

"So?" Aura says. "What's been going on around here lately?"

"Bones are being stolen," I say.

"Exactly," she says. "I think someone is trying to reanimate these dead people."

"Yuck," Hairball says.

"But that's not all," she says. "You'll never guess who wrote the book?"

Everyone looks at one another.

"Donald Duck?" Hairball guesses.

"No," Aura says. "Professor Claude Faustius."

My fork slips from my hand and clangs on my plate.

"Seriously?" I say. "The Black Magic guy?"

"Yep," she says. "He published it a few years ago."

"Maybe that's why he doesn't teach here anymore?" Rage says. "I bet Van Helsing didn't approve of that."

"That's probably why his office is locked up," I say. "So nobody can get inside to see what he did."

"But here's the thing," Aura says. "There are two volumes to the Alchemy of Reanimation. I could only find the first one in Van Helsing's library. The second volume is the one that actually tells you how to bring the dead back to life. I bet it's inside Faustius' office. I bet there's a clue in there about those grave robbers too."

"But we can't get in there," Rage says. "It says 'Entry Forbidden,' remember? Plus, it's locked up like crazy."

"Maybe for you," Aura says smiling, "but not for a ghost."

VAN HELSING ACADEMY

STUDENT ASSESSMENT

VITALS:
NAME: Harry Woolsey
EYES: Brown
HAIR: Brown
HEIGHT: 6'1"
WEIGHT: 205 lbs

NOTES: Yeti-DNA provides incredible strength and heightened sense of smell. Not very mobile and could become a large target. Requires a lot of food.

CODENAME: Hairball

CLASSIFICATION TYPE:
Abnormal – Yeti

SUPERNATURAL ASSESSMENT:

STRENGTH	●●●●○
AGILITY	●○○○○
FIGHTING	●●●●○
INTELLECT	●●●○○
CONTROL	●●●○○

TEACHABLE?	Yes	No
VAN HELSING	●	○
CRAWLER	●	○
HOLMWOOD	●	○
SEWARD	●	○
MORRIS	●	○
HEXUM	○	●
FAUSTIUS	●	○

RISK LEVEL: LOW

CHAPTER TWELVE

CREEPIN' IT REAL

I can't believe we're doing this.

I mean, we were just punished by Van Helsing last night! Yet, here we are, hiding in a row of thorny hedges, risking our necks on another one of Aura's crazy hunches. If we're caught it probably means the end of our little gang, but we've got to find out the truth. After all, there are just too many strange things going on.

First, zombies are digging up graves and stealing the bones of dead people. Then, Aura discovers that creepy book in Van Helsing's private library about bringing the dead back to life.

Are they related?

Maybe. Maybe not.

But here's the kicker.

The book was written by Professor Claude Faustius. The very same Professor Claude Faustius who used to teach Black Magic right here at the Van Helsing Academy. The very same Professor Claude Faustius whose office is in lockdown mode.

More than a coincidence?

Yeah, I'd buy that.

So, that's why we're camped out here in the bushes. Well, at least Rage, Stanphibian, Hairball, and I are camped out in the bushes. We're waiting for all of the teachers to go home so we can break into Faustius' office and solve the mystery once and for all.

Aura is on lookout duty, floating high above the main building. InvisiBill is stationed inside, scouting out the professors. The rest of us are stuffed inside this thicket, way too close for anyone's comfort.

Yet, surprisingly, everything is going smoothly.

At least, so far.

Getting by Vi Clops was pretty simple. All we had to do was deliver another dozen pizzas and she was down for the count. I never knew outwitting a cyclops would be so easy, but according to Aura I still have lots to learn.

We just need the professors to go home for the night. Since they keep different hours we brainstormed ideas on how to get them all out of the building at once. InvisiBill wanted to pull the fire alarm but we told him not to do it as it would just raise suspicions. I hope he listens.

In the end, we agreed our best option was to just wait them out. Which probably means we're stuck here for a while.

Suddenly, a horrific, fishy smell assaults my nostrils.

"Ugh! What's that?" Hairball whispers.

"Sorry," Stanphibian says.

"Seriously?" Rage whispers. "Are you trying to put me back in the infirmary?"

Before going on this crazy adventure, we debated if Rage should even come along. After all, he's supposed to be resting. But after arguing with each other for a whole thirty-minutes, Rage told us he was coming no matter what so that was a complete waste of time.

I look up at the cupola to see if Aura is giving us any signals, but she's facing the other way, keeping an eye out for unexpected stragglers. She sort of looks other-worldly in the moonlight, kind of like a guardian angel.

Just then, something comes crashing through the brush, knocking me and Hairball on our backsides.

"Hey!" Hairball yells.

"Shut it, fluffy cakes," InvisiBill whispers. "They're coming."

I glance up at Aura. She gives a thumbs up and phases through the wall.

Someone is exiting the building.

"No noises," I whisper, "from any body parts."

Just then, Holmwood and Morris step through the doors.

I'm the closest to the stairs, so I have the best vantage point. The two professors are having an intense conversation, but instead of heading over to the Faculty Residence Hall, they stop on the front porch.

What's going on? Why aren't they leaving?

They're speaking in low tones. I tilt my head, trying to make out what they're saying.

"—long did he say he'd be gone?" Professor Holmwood asks.

"He didn't," Professor Morris answers. "I offered to ride along, but he looked like he had a burr in his saddle and said he needed to go alone. All I could do was insist he take some special equipment with him. There wasn't much else I could do."

"He's so stubborn," Professor Holmwood says. "I certainly hope he's careful. This is a dangerous appointment with a most unsavory character."

"Like a snake in the grass," Professor Morris says.

"Please, Quincy," Professor Holmwood says, "if you hear anything, anything at all, let me know."

"Of course, Lucy," Professor Morris says. "Fortunately, he's a very competent fellow."

"Yes," she says. "That's precisely why I'm worried."

"Well, I'm going to take my evening stroll," Professor Morris says. "Would you like to join me?"

"No thank you," she says. "I need to do some lesson planning for tomorrow. It's skin-rider day."

"Exhilarating," he says, tipping his hat. "Well, goodnight."

"Goodnight," Professor Holmwood says.

Then, they go their separate ways.

"What was that all about?" Rage whispers.

"I have no idea," I answer.

"Shhh!" InvisiBill interjects. "Shut up."

Just then, Professor Seward exits the building carrying a tall stack of test booklets. I bet my 'monsters in the medieval era' pop quiz is in that pile. He's probably grading them tonight. Boy, did I screw that one up.

Suddenly, a strong wind kicks up out of nowhere, blowing several booklets from the top of his pile onto the front porch.

"Unbelievable," Professor Seward mutters.

As he bends over to pick them up, I spot something out of the corner of my eye and my heart stops beating. One of the booklets blew off the porch and landed right next to my foot! If Seward reaches into the bushes to get it, we'll be caught!

"HOOT! HOOT!"

Huh? What's that? It sounded like an owl caught in a blender somewhere high above.

"HOOT!" it repeats.

All of us look up, including Professor Seward.

And then, "SCOOT!"

Scoot? What bird says—?

Suddenly, I feel like a world-class dufus.

It's Aura! She's making a distraction.

I snatch the booklet and toss it back on the porch. Right on cue, Professor Seward scoops it up with all the others and goes merrily on his way.

Whew! That was close.

Now there's just one left.

The one I'm most worried about.

I hear Hexum before I see him, the TAPPING of his walking stick announcing his arrival. I hold my breath as he makes his way across the front porch.

C'mon. Keep going. Keep going.

Hexum walks down the front steps.

Yes!

He steps onto the driveway.

Yes! Yes! Yes!

And then he stops.

No! No! No!

Hexum stands there, his cape billowing in the wind.

What's he doing? Why isn't he leaving?

Then, he turns and my heart skips a beat!

He's staring into the bushes!

I freeze.

Does he see us? Is he looking at me?

I don't know what to do.

"HOOT!"

That's Aura! She's creating another diversion.

"HOOT!"

Hexum looks up and smiles. "A hoot indeed," he says loudly. Then, he extends his walking stick and continues on his way.

No one moves until he's clearly out of sight.

"Thank heavens," Rage whispers, collapsing onto my back. "I thought we were going to die."

"Stop yapping and get up," Hairball whispers.

"Before we do die."

After that, all of our best-laid plans for a 'slow and stealthy' break-in are chucked out the window. We race inside the building and book over to the faculty wing. Thankfully, no one is around. Nevertheless, I keep my eyes peeled for any of Crawler's critters who might report us via the world wide web.

Eventually, we reach Faustius' office and skid to a stop. After crashing into InvisiBill, I take a quick count. We're all here, except for one. Where's Aura?

Just then, a pair of legs materializes through the ceiling over our heads.

"Ahhh!" Rage screams.

Aura lands smack in the middle of us.

Suddenly, there's a loud BEEPING noise. We go into panic mode, trying to find the source.

"It's Rage's blood pressure watch," InvisiBill says.

"Turn it off!" Hairball orders.

"I can't!" Rage says. "There's no off button!"

"Give me that," Hairball says, ripping it off of Rage's wrist and crushing it in his hand. "There's your off button."

"Ow!" Rage says, rubbing his arm. "Did you have to take half my skin with it? And Aura, seriously? Was that necessary?"

"Sorry," Aura says. "I took a shortcut after making sure Hexum was gone."

"Hexum may be gone," Hairball says. "But what

about Van Helsing?"

We look down the hallway. Van Helsing's door is closed, but that doesn't mean he's not inside.

"I think he's gone," Rage says. "Didn't you hear what Holmwood and Morris were talking about? They said he went out for some kind of dangerous appointment."

"But they never said his name," InvisiBill adds. "Maybe it was Crawler and not Van Helsing?"

"Only one way to find out," I say, making my way down the hall.

I put my ear against the door. There aren't any noises coming from inside, not even a crackling fire. Then, I realize the door is cool to the touch.

"He's not there," I say.

"Are you sure?" Hairball asks. "Maybe Aura should phase in there."

"No need," I say. "I think we're good to go."

"Then let's get this over with," Rage says. "Before someone shows up."

We hustle back to Faustius' door. With seven locks and one 'Entry Forbidden' sign, Van Helsing couldn't have been any clearer.

"Are you sure you want to do this?" I ask Aura.

"Really, Bram?" she says, rolling her eyes.

Then, she steps straight through the door.

"Okay, this is really happening," Rage says, his head in his hands.

"I'll keep a lookout," InvisiBill says, his footsteps echoing down the hallway. "But make it snappy."

Making it snappy sounds great, but there's nothing the rest of us can do but wait. I mean, Aura's been inside only a few seconds, but it already feels like an eternity. That's when I realize we haven't heard from her.

I lean against the door. "Aura, can you hear me?"

But there's no response.

I knock hard. "Aura?"

"Cut it out!" comes her muffled voice. "I hear you. I'm just getting my bearings. It's dark in here."

Whew! She's safe.

"Can you see at all?" I ask, this time much quieter.

"A little," she says. "Some light is filtering through a boarded-up window, but that's about it. This place is big-time creepy and there's all sorts of scientific equipment in here. Microscopes and test tubes and beakers. Is that an operating table? Oh, yuck!"

"What? What is it?"

"Sorry," she says. "I-I think there's a whole shelf of brains. So gross."

"Do you see a book?" I ask. "Remember, that's what we're looking for."

"I know what we're looking for," she says. "I'm not a moron. Wait, here's a desk with all sorts of— Hang on! There's a book on it! Let me read the spine. Yes! This is it! The Alchemy of Reanimation Volume II! Let me see if I can open it somehow and—"

Suddenly, there's silence.

"Aura?"

No answer.

We all look at one another.

"Okay," Hairball says. "Where'd she go?"

"Aura?" I yell, knocking on the door. "Aura, are you okay? Aura?"

There's no reply.

"Something happened!" I say. "Hairball, bust it down!"

"But we'll get caught!" InvisiBill says. He must have come back down the hall.

"Dude, who cares?" I say. "Aura's in trouble. Take it down, Hairball!"

The furry giant rears back his fist and pounds the door. The next thing I know, Hairball is flying backward through the air, crashing into the opposite wall.

"That's Black Magic!" Rage says. "The door must be cursed!"

"Pull off the locks!" I say.

Stanphibian grabs a lock and tugs with all of his might, but it won't break off.

"Forget it," InvisiBill says. "We can't get inside. We've got to get the professors. Stanphibian, let's go!"

The two of them take off, but I have a feeling we can't waste time waiting for help to arrive. Aura is in trouble now! I pound on the door again.

"Aura! Are you okay? Are you still there? Aura?"

Still nothing.

I've got to help her. But how?

Then, I spin around and my eyes land on Hexum's door. Suddenly, I hear his voice inside my head:

'If you are truly going to be a Supernatural, you must learn to think like a Supernatural.'

He's right. That's the only way I'll ever believe in things I can't imagine.

While Rage is helping Hairball back to his feet, I close my eyes, tuning them out. I focus on one thought.

How can I best help Aura?

Suddenly, I envision a vapor cloud flowing beneath the crack of a door.

That's it! If we can't go through Faustius' door, maybe I can go around it?

I fixate on that vapor cloud.

I hold that image in my mind.

I focus everything I can on that image.

A cloud of mist.

Then, I start to believe.

Suddenly, I'm tingly all over.

I feel light—lighter than air.

My entire body feels like it's spreading out. Like my molecules are pulling apart!

"Um, Bram?" comes Rage's voice. It sounds distant.

I feel like I'm floating, like I'm high in the air, brushing against the ceiling. But my body feels scattered. Like I've dissipated into a gazillion, tiny particles.

I see Rage and Hairball looking up at me, their mouths hanging wide open.

I… did it?

"Bram, is that you?" Rage asks.

But I can't answer him.

First, I have no mouth.

Second, my thoughts are on Aura.

I've got to help her.

I focus my mind, clustering my atoms together.

Then, I flow through the cracks of Faustius' door.

VAN HELSING ACADEMY

STUDENT ASSESSMENT

VITALS:
NAME: Stanley Seawald
EYES: Black
HAIR: Green
HEIGHT: 4'7"
WEIGHT: 101 lbs

NOTES: Can breathe underwater, limited breathing on land. Quick reflexes, excellent swimmer, super strong skin. Rarely speaks.

CODENAME: Stanphibian

CLASSIFICATION TYPE:
Abnormal – Gill-man

SUPERNATURAL ASSESSMENT:

STRENGTH	●●●○○
AGILITY	●●●●●
FIGHTING	●●●○○
INTELLECT	●●●○○
CONTROL	●●●●○

TEACHABLE?	Yes	No
VAN HELSING	●	○
CRAWLER	●	○
HOLMWOOD	●	○
SEWARD	●	○
MORRIS	●	○
HEXUM	○	●
FAUSTIUS	○	●

RISK LEVEL: LOW

CHAPTER THIRTEEN

WELL, THAT SUCKS

As I drift into Faustius' office, I know I need to be ready for anything.

I also learn that maintaining my mist-form is tricky business. Half of me is hugging the ceiling while the other half is skimming the floor. I need to stay focused to keep my particles together, and after a few seconds of excruciating mental effort, I manage to pull myself into a fairly respectable vapor cloud.

It's dark in here, just as Aura said, but fortunately, I can still see even in mist form. And to my surprise, one major benefit of being a mist is that I can see in multiple directions at once.

The only problem is that I don't see Aura anywhere. Where is she?

At first, I feel a flutter of panic, but then I realize I've got this. After all, I've paid attention in Professor Morris' class about Supernatural crime scene investigations. Now I just have to apply what I've learned. So, here goes.

Step one, secure the crime scene. Well, it appears I'm

the only one here so a big check mark for that one. Step two, sweep the crime scene, assess the environment, and look for clues. Okay, if I want to cover the most space in the fastest time possible I'll need to fan out.

That's kind of frustrating after working so hard to pull myself together, but what other choice do I have? So, I relax my concentration and feel myself spreading apart. The good news is that it only takes a few seconds to permeate the room. The bad news is that Faustius' office is as creepy as Aura said it was. Maybe even creepier.

I run down the list of what Aura reported seeing. Brains on a shelf. Check. Bizarre operating table. Check. Feeling totally freaked out. Double check.

But there's still no sign of Aura.

I wish I knew what step three of a Supernatural investigation was, but we haven't gotten that far yet.

Maybe Aura is just playing a practical joke, like when we tried tracking her with the Spirit Sensor. She's probably back at Monster House laughing her head off. Boy, that would be great. But I know it's not true.

Something happened to her.

Something bad.

Part of me feels like I should head back into the hallway, but I know it's fear talking. Aura needs my help and hovering like a cloud isn't going to get me any closer to solving this mystery. I need to get my sneakers on the ground. I just hope I can change back to normal, otherwise, I'll be stuck like this forever and get a code name like "Gas Boy" or something.

I concentrate hard, picturing myself as a regular kid. I put all of my focus on that mental image. Then, I start to feel tingly again, like my atoms are coming back together. I feel myself becoming heavier, more solid.

The next thing I know, I'm falling from the ceiling!

I SLAM hard on my backside and roll over.

Note to self: the next time I transition from mist to human form, make sure I'm near the floor.

Suddenly, I hear KNOCKING.

"Bram, are you okay!" comes Rage's voice.

"I'm good!" I yell. "Just fell from the ceiling. Only hurt my pride. I don't see Aura though!"

"Maybe you should get out of there," Rage says. "The guys are trying to find Van Helsing or Crawler. Let's let them handle it."

"There's no time!" I yell back. I have a bad feeling that if I can't figure out what happened to Aura, she'll be lost forever. I spin around the room. What was she doing when we last heard from her? Then, I remember.

The book!

It was on Faustius' desk.

Where the heck is that desk?

I'm about to make a mad scramble when I suddenly feel drained. Changing into a cloud and back again sapped my energy. But I can't stop now. I need to find that book.

Suddenly, I notice a piece of furniture sticking out from behind the shelf of brains. For some reason, I missed this area. So, I head over to explore.

Bingo! It's a desk alright.

It's positioned beneath a boarded window. The surface is large, and every square inch is covered with beakers, microscopes, and... a book!

Just then, I notice something shimmery on the floor.

It's Aura's badge!

Okay, that's not a good sign.

I pick it up and shove it into my pocket. Then, I get back to the book. It's thick, with a tattered black cover and yellowed pages. It's still closed, so I guess Aura never got it open. I check out the text on the spine. It reads:

THE ALCHEMY OF REANIMATION
VOLUME II
BY PROFESSOR CLAUDE FAUSTIUS

This is it!

I reach for it but then stop myself.

Aura was opening it when something happened to her—and she's a ghost! Maybe I shouldn't open it. I mean, if doors and locks can be cursed then who knows what kind of Black Magic is inside of this thing? Yet, this book is definitely linked to Aura's disappearance.

I just don't know how.

What should I do?

The way I see it, I have two options. Option one, leave the book here and mist my way out of Faustius' office for help. Since Van Helsing put the locks on Faustius' door, he'd know how to open them up so we could get back inside. The risk is that he's probably not around. I mean, according to Holmwood and Morris, he left the Academy for his appointment a long time ago. Plus, we'd lose precious time finding Aura.

Option two, stay in kid form, grab the book, and break out of Faustius' office. That way, even if Van Helsing isn't here, we can track him down and hand deliver the book as quickly as possible. The risk is that I'll have to ensure no one opens the book. Especially InvisiBill because he'd be the one to do something stupid like that. The problem is that I'm not sure I can unlock Faustius' door from the inside. After all, it's cursed.

Decisions, decisions.

Okay, option two it is!

I grab the book, and immediately I know it's a mistake! There's a strong force pulling me forward like I'm being sucked inside a vacuum cleaner!

What's going on?

I try releasing the book, but it won't let me go!

I'm slip—

***

I wake up in a fog.

I try opening my eyes, but my head is pounding so hard even my eyelids hurt. Nevertheless, as soon as I pry them open, I wish I hadn't, because it only takes a second to realize I'm in trouble. Serious trouble.

I'm in some kind of a circular chamber with stone walls along the perimeter and a domed, leaded-glass ceiling. Looking up, I see it's still nighttime, but not a star is hanging in the sky. All around me are various stations holding strange sciency stuff, like giant microscopes, bubbling beakers, and electric amps. To my left are two metal tables complete with wrist and ankle shackles. A small table between them holds an array of surgical tools, like scalpels, knives, and scissors.

By the looks of it, I'd say I'm in some mad scientist's laboratory, and that's probably not a good thing.

How did I end up here? Then, it hits me.

The book!

The last thing I remember is grabbing Faustius' book. Suddenly, it dawns on me that I'm not holding it anymore. Where did it go? I need to get that book to Van Helsing before it's too late to save Aura!

It's not until I get to my feet that I realize I won't be saving anyone anytime soon. That's because I'm standing inside a glass tube exactly like the one Hexum created in my mind, except this one is real and completely sealed at the top and bottom, making escaping in mist form impossible.

Not that I could turn into a mist anyway. I'm so wiped out I feel like I could sleep for days. Plus, I'm absolutely starving, which I've learned is never a good thing for a vampire like me.

I look around as best I can, but I don't see Faustius' book anywhere. I feel like such a dope. Clearly, you didn't have to open the book to be zapped by its curse. And the Black Magic must be powerful enough to work on ghosts too. So, Aura must be around here somewhere.

"Aura?" I yell, my voice echoing in the tube.

No answer.

Well, I can't stay trapped in here forever. Maybe I can knock this tube over and break it open? I lean up against one side of the glass and then launch myself against the other, pushing with all of my might, but the tube doesn't budge. I do, however, manage to bruise my shoulder.

Monster fail.

I've got to get out of here.

Just then, I hear a CREAK behind me.

"Aura?"

But instead of Aura, I'm suddenly facing two werewolves—one is red and the other is black! Where'd they come from? Fortunately, we're separated by glass, but they're looking at me like I'm some kind of a zoo animal. Shouldn't the roles be reversed?

"Hi guys," I say casually. "Great to see you. Hey, any chance you can spring me and let me walk out of here alive? Promise I'll get you all the dog chow you can eat."

The red one bares his teeth and ROARS.

"Okay," I say quickly. "Forget the dog food. Think

steaks. Thick, juicy steaks every night for the rest of your lives? Not bad, huh? I'll even throw in a bottomless salad bowl."

"Don't waste your breath," comes a voice. "You know you can't control them. You don't have the power."

I turn to find a hunched, bald man standing between the operating tables. His dark, beady eyes stare at me through gold-rimmed glasses, and he's wearing a white lab coat and cradling something in his arms.

"Who are you?" I ask.

"Who do you think I am?" the bent man answers.

I know I've never seen him before. But he has a distinct accent. It sounds different than Van Helsing's accent. Maybe… German? Then, I notice what he's holding.

It's a bundle of bones!

There's a skull, a femur, a collar bone…

Then, it hits me!

"Y-You're Professor Faustius!"

But Faustius doesn't respond. Instead, he carefully lays the bones down on one of the metal tables. Then, he reaches beneath and pulls out a bin filled with even more bones. After laying those out, he grabs another bin and then repeats this several more times. Minutes later, he's organized a complete skeleton.

This is weird. Where'd he get all those…

Suddenly, it all comes together.

Those must be the stolen bones!

"You robbed those graves!" I exclaim.

"Guess you caught me red-handed," Faustius says, waving a hand bone. "Allow me to introduce our guest. The legs, arms, and torso belonged to a man named Jonah Covington, a four-time Olympic gold medalist in the decathlon who set world records in the 100-meter sprint, long jump, high jump, javelin throw, and pole vault. The bones of the hands, wrists, and fingers belonged to a man named Lloyd McAdams, the most decorated sharpshooter in military history. And the skull belonged to a gentleman named Dr. Eugene Albert, Nobel prize winner in physics."

"Okay," I say, totally freaked out. "You have some really stiff friends."

"Perhaps," he says. "But they won't stay that way for long."

Okay, this guy is nuts. What he's planning to do with that skeleton is beyond me, but I don't want to stick around to find out. I've got to get out of here. I need a plan. Maybe I can bluff my way out.

"You might as well let me go," I say. "Van Helsing is on his way right now."

"Really?" Faustius says. "How could Van Helsing find us here, in the middle of nowhere?" He lifts a femur. "Are you pulling my leg?"

"No," I say. "He followed me here."

Then, I realize I made a big mistake. After all, I didn't exactly come here voluntarily. Faustius' cursed book sent me here.

"Your survival skills are very poor," Faustius says. "Hexum has not trained you well but I'm not surprised. That pompous bore took far more credit than he deserved. But I'm afraid your ruse is ineffective. For one, I have cast a spell banishing any of Crawler's eight-legged sentries from my lair. But even more importantly, I know for a fact that Van Helsing will not be coming to save you. We had an appointment to meet somewhere else."

An appointment? So Faustius was the person Van Helsing left the academy to meet? Now I know why Professor Holmwood was so nervous. This guy is a total wackadoo.

"Unfortunately, my invitation was only a decoy," Faustius continues. "Soon, we will no longer need to worry about your Headmaster."

"What?" I say. "What does that mean?"

"It means that several of my associates are waiting to greet him," Faustius says with a smirk. "I would have so enjoyed seeing the terror in his eyes as he's ripped limb from limb. But alas, I have other priorities."

"You're going to kill him?" I say, my voice rising.

"Are you fond of Van Helsing?" he asks. "I'm not surprised. I know firsthand how manipulative he can be. I'm sure he told you many false stories about the Dark Ones, portraying them as evil."

"They killed my parents!" I say.

"Did they?" Faustius says calmly. "Do you know that

for a fact? Or are you merely taking his word for it?"

His words catch me off guard.

"I know the Dark Ones are evil!" I snap back. "Van Helsing told me they're searching for the Blood Grail to bring Count Dracula back to life. I'd call that pretty evil."

"Perhaps you should understand both sides of the story before passing judgment on what is evil and what is not," Faustius says, walking towards me. "Yes, the Dark Ones are searching for the Blood Grail, but they are doing so for noble reasons. And I am leading them."

"Wait a second," I say. "You're a Dark One?"

"Not just any Dark One," he says, brushing the werewolves aside. "I am the High Lord of the Dark Ones."

"Th-The High Lord?" I stutter. "You mean, like, the person in charge? No wonder Van Helsing threw you out of the academy. You're a monster!"

Faustius puts a hand on the glass and smiles.

"And by coincidence, so are you," Faustius says. "Are you aware of how monsters were treated before the reign of Count Dracula?"

Suddenly, I remember Professor Seward's lectures about the great monster hunts, like the Zombie Crusades and the Werewolf Inquisition.

"They were persecuted," Faustius continues, "hunted down and destroyed by angry mobs of Naturals led by some Van Helsing ancestor or another. Their thirst for Supernatural blood was insatiable. It did not matter if you were a man or a woman, an adult or a child. Sometimes, it didn't matter if you were a monster at all. So, tell me, who are the real monsters now?"

I think about Aura, Rage, and even InvisiBill.

I couldn't imagine them being chased down.

Hunted.

"And now, here we are again," Faustius says, "with yet another Van Helsing leading the charge. But instead of angry mobs, this one is using Supernatural children to destroy other Supernaturals. It's a novel approach, but should we simply stand by and let history repeat itself? I don't think so. Instead, let's create a world where Supernaturals live in peace."

I'm confused. For some reason, he's making sense.

"It's all within our reach, Bram," Faustius says. "You see, because your great-grandfather was not a vampire, he only succeeded in destroying Count Dracula's mortal body. But Count Dracula's spirit wasn't destroyed. It lives on. That is why he can be resurrected. That is why he can be returned to life. And with my steady hand guiding him, we can show humanity that Supernaturals are once again the superior race."

Superior race? Hold on a second!

"You're nuts," I say. "That's wrong!"

"Is it?" Faustius says. "Is it any more wrong than what Van Helsing has planned for you?"

"What are you talking about?" I say.

"You mean, you don't know?" Faustius says, his

right eyebrow rising. "Are you saying your trustworthy Headmaster didn't tell you?"

"Tell me?" I say. "Tell me what?"

"Please, Bram," he says, looking into my eyes. "Heed my words, because unlike Van Helsing, you can trust me to always tell you the truth. Van Helsing may have told you that you are the last of the vampires, but I fear he neglected to tell you what that means."

"What are you talking about?" I ask, my heart racing.

"I am sorry, Bram," he says. "But only a vampire can truly kill another vampire."

Wait, what?

Van Helsing never told me that.

"W-What are you saying?" I ask, fearing the answer.

"Don't you see?" Faustius says. "Van Helsing is using you. Because you are half-vampire, Van Helsing is planning to sacrifice your life to destroy Count Dracula."

CHAPTER FOURTEEN

THE FACE OF EVIL

I'm utterly speechless.

I mean, this Faustius guy just dropped a bomb on me. First, he tells me only a vampire can truly kill another vampire. That's some pretty important information that Van Helsing forgot to mention. Then, Faustius claims Van Helsing is just using me to destroy Count Dracula—and he's willing to sacrifice my life in the process!

Why didn't Van Helsing tell me that? Was he afraid I'd run away? Or is Faustius just blowing smoke?

For a second, I don't know who to believe.

But then I remember Faustius saying he's the High Lord of the Dark Ones, the evil group that killed my parents. Plus, he confirmed the Dark Ones are still searching for the Blood Grail so they can bring Count Dracula back to life. And to top it off, he's got me trapped in his crazy laboratory.

I'd say that's three strikes.

Winner—Van Helsing.

I need to keep Faustius talking until I find a way out.

"Why are you so angry with Van Helsing anyway?" I ask. "What did he do to you?"

"He betrayed me," Faustius says, his lips quivering.

Wow, I can tell whatever happened between those two is still really bugging him. I need to keep him distracted. "What do you mean?" I say.

"If you must know, it all began decades ago," Faustius says, his eyes drifting into space. "At that time, I was just a boy, orphaned and alone, working as a clerk in the town library. For a hard day's work, I was paid in bread and allowed to sleep on the cold basement floor. Everyone assumed I was stupid, but I knew I had special talents. I had a gift for languages, and I was fascinated by books. They were my escape. My sanctuary."

Faustius heads towards the metal tables.

"At night, after everyone would leave, I would read by candlelight, consuming book after book, always wishing for a more adventurous life like my heroes in the great stories. And then, one day, almost by accident, I stumbled across a dusty book lodged beneath a bookcase. I had never seen it before. Its cloth cover was tattered, and the pages inside had strange letters and intricate drawings. It captivated me, and I wondered what this odd book was about."

For some reason, a chill runs down my spine.

"It took me months to decode it," he continues, "translating each page letter by letter, word by word. I quickly realized it wasn't a story at all, but rather an ancient book of Black Magic. I studied it carefully, committing every incantation to memory, but I was too timid to try any of them myself."

Okay, maybe getting him talking wasn't such a good idea because this is getting weirder by the minute.

"Until one day," Faustius says, his eyes narrowing. "I was sweeping the alleyway when I was accosted by a group of privileged and bored teenagers. I tried to ignore them, but they persisted. Things quickly turned physical, and they left me in a broken heap. As I stumbled back into the library, I swore things would be different from that day forward. I pulled out the book of Black Magic, turned to an entry entitled 'Spell of Summoning,' and carefully followed the instructions. Then, to my astonishment, a small creature appeared before me."

"Wait, what?" I blurt out.

"He was as big as a puppy," Faustius says, "with red skin, little horns and big, black eyes. Without uttering a sound, he left the library, and when he returned, I knew exactly what he had done. He had avenged me, and in return, I took him in. I hid him in the basement, never revealing his existence to anyone."

Okay, this guy is legitimately cuckoo. I rub my hands along the glass, looking for any crack I can mist out of, but it's perfectly smooth.

"Over time we grew close," Faustius continues. "I was the master and he was my pet. But things got out of hand. He would disappear often, and bad things began happening around town with greater frequency. I quickly realized he took joy in causing others misery. And as he grew bigger, his appetite for destruction grew larger. I didn't know what to do. So, I prayed for a miracle. And one evening, it came. There was a knock at my door."

Faustius picks up a scalpel. What's that for?

"Van Helsing was a younger man back then," he says, "he was carrying a knapsack and asked if he could come inside. He said he could help me with my problem. Of course, I had no other solution, so I let him in. We waited up all night until my creature returned home. Upon seeing it, Van Helsing wasted no time before destroying it with a silver arrow. To my surprise, he had concealed a crossbow in his knapsack, and in the blink of an eye, my problem was solved. And my only friend in the world was gone."

Wow, I can tell he's still heartbroken over this.

"You know, I was in a similar situation once," I say. "One of my foster families had a hamster, but it got free and we never saw it again. Guess who got blamed for that one?"

"Do not belittle me, child," Faustius says, gripping the scalpel tightly. "I was furious. Van Helsing called my pet a 'demon' and demanded to know how it was conjured. That is when I showed him my book. Van Helsing was both surprised and impressed by my talent. He asked if I would be interested in becoming his apprentice at a special school he was starting. I was shocked. Me? A poor boy joining a prestigious academy? I couldn't believe it. Of course, I agreed at once, but I never forgave him for what he did."

I can see the anger seething in Faustius' eyes.

"Van Helsing took me under his wing," Faustius continues. "I helped him establish his academy and recruit his other professors. But as I grew older, I knew I had more to offer. I begged him to make me a professor, but he refused. He would not admit it, but I knew he was afraid of what I might teach the children. It wasn't until I threatened to leave that he finally relented. I should have been happy. After all, I had finally achieved my goal. But instead, I felt hollow. It was then I realized Van Helsing never respected me. Since the day we met, he kept me close not because he liked me, but because he wanted to keep an eye on me."

I don't blame him.

"And then one night," Faustius says, "I had a dream. I realized I no longer needed to stand in Van Helsing's shadow. If he could build a school, I could build an empire. If he could teach monsters to live in society, I could teach them to dominate society. My power was stifled under Van Helsing's thumb. But to pull off my ambition, I needed operatives. So, I rekindled the Dark Ones right under Van Helsing's nose."

"You're a maniac!" I say.

"Perhaps I am," he says, approaching me, scalpel in hand. "Or perhaps I'm a visionary. When Van Helsing got wind of my plans, he forced me out of the academy. Fortunately, I escaped before he uncovered my true purpose—to capture Count Dracula's spirit and bring him back to life."

Spirit?

OMG! I almost forgot.

"Where's Aura?" I demand. "What did you do with her."

"Ah, your little ghost friend," Faustius says with a wicked smile. "I'm afraid she has left us."

"Left us?" I say. "What do you mean?"

"I mean she's gone," Faustius says. "She was a ghost, remember? Like all ghosts trapped on earth, she had a mission to complete. And now that her mission is done, her soul was released to the great beyond."

"What are you talking about?" I ask, totally confused. "What mission?"

"You *are* a naïve one, aren't you?" Faustius says, now standing on the other side of the glass. "Her mission was simple—to bring you to me."

"Liar!" I yell.

"I wish I were lying," Faustius says. "But again, I will only tell you the truth. Your friend was merely a pawn in this game of monsters. You see, one day, while I was traveling in the city, I witnessed her unfortunate demise. It was a terrible accident; one she never saw coming. Nevertheless, I was able to capture her soul with a simple spell before it left."

I shudder. Poor Aura.

"Through this spell, I could control her actions," Faustius continues. "Of course, she was none the wiser. I knew her powers may come in handy one day, perhaps as a spy, so I enrolled her in the academy. At the time I did not realize she would become such a valuable asset."

Faustius twirls the scalpel in his fingers.

"But after several failed efforts to capture you directly," he says, shooting annoyed looks at the werewolves. "I had to take a subtler approach. So, I used your ghost friend to lure you here."

My mind races into overdrive. I mean, Aura was the one who led us to that cemetery with the grave robbers and werewolves in the first place. She also discovered Faustius' book in Van Helsing's library. And it was her idea to break into Faustius' office. Could he be right? Was Faustius manipulating her the whole time?

And was this the reason she was still stuck here? I feel like I've been punched in the gut. I mean, she was my friend. Maybe my best friend. And now… she's gone.

"I hate you!" I scream.

"That's sad," Faustius says. "I was hoping we could work together."

"Never!" I yell.

"Very well," he says. "Have it your way."

Then, his mouth starts moving, but he's speaking so low I can't hear what he's saying. His lips are forming the same patterns repeatedly, like he's chanting. Then, I realize, he's putting a spell on me!

Suddenly, my whole body tightens up.

I can't move a muscle!

What's happening?

"Struggling is futile," he says, "I have employed a Curse of Immobility. You will be unable to move or use any vampire tricks. However, I have allowed you the ability to breathe and to speak if you wish. In case you change your mind before it's too late."

"No way!" I yell.

This is ridiculous, my arms and legs are locked in place. I can't move at all.

"There is no chance for escape now," Faustius says. Then, he snaps his fingers and my glass prison is gone! The werewolves grab my arms and lift me into the air.

"Wait, what are you doing?" I protest.

"Don't worry," Faustius says, "this part will be quick and relatively painless."

I want to fight back, but I can only watch as the werewolves carry me towards the metal tables.

Strangely, Faustius is busy fitting a robe around the skeleton. "There, now you are dressed. That will save any embarrassment."

"What are you doing?" I ask.

"Preparing the bones," Faustius says. "It's the respectable thing to do after I reanimate them with Count Dracula's spirit."

Reanimate?

Wait a minute! He's actually going to try this? But instead of using Count Dracula's bones, he's going to use the bones of these dead heroes. If he pulls this off, Count Dracula will be smarter and stronger than ever!

The werewolves lay me down on the empty table, shackling my wrists and ankles. Okay, I've seen enough horror movies to know where this is heading.

My heart is racing.

"Let me go!" I demand.

"Sorry, but no," he says. "I've worked too hard to acquire you. You see, you play a pivotal role in my plans. Plans that begin right now."

Faustius closes his eyes and begins chanting in a language I've never heard before. It's another spell but based on his reddening complexion this one is taking a big toll on him.

I can't understand what he's saying, except for one word I keep hearing over and over again.

DRACUL.

Suddenly, there's a loud CRASH overhead, and when I look up, I see shards of glass falling from above. There's a giant hole in the domed ceiling, and cold air is flooding into the room.

But Faustius just keeps on chanting, his voice rising louder and louder.

Just then, a black mist swirls over my body, setting the hairs on the back of my neck on end.

"W-What's that?" I ask.

But deep down, I know the answer.

The black cloud circulates throughout the room, leaving a trail of darkness in its wake. And as it passes over me again, I'm overcome by a wave of negativity.

"Yes!" Faustius screams, his eyes wide with delight. "He is here! The King of Darkness is finally here!"

The King of Darkness?

Dracula's spirit is here!

But then I remember there's no Blood Grail. When Aura told Dracula's tale back in Professor Seward's class, the Dark Ones needed the Blood Grail to restore him to life. But Faustius told me he's still searching for it. So, I don't know how he thinks he's gonna pull this off.

"These are great parlor tricks," I say, "but let's face it, you still haven't found the Blood Grail. So why don't we stop this whole thing before somebody loses an eye."

Suddenly, Faustius stands over me, scalpel in hand.

"I'm afraid you couldn't be more wrong," he says. "My quest for the Blood Grail has finally ended."

Then, I notice he's holding a golden chalice!

Oh no. It can't be.

"I-Is that the Blood Grail?" I stammer.

"No," he says, laughing. "This is merely a cup."

"So, you don't have it!" I say relieved.

"You still don't understand, do you?" Faustius says. "You are the last of the vampires. Dracula's Supernatural blood is flowing through your veins. Bram, the Blood Grail is you."

CLASSIFIED

Person(s) of Interest

CODE NAME: None

REAL NAME: CLAUDE FAUSTIUS

BASE OF OPERATIONS: CURRENTLY UNKNOWN

Category: Natural

Sub-Type: Not Applicable

Height: 5'9"

Weight: 175 lbs

FACTS: Faustius is a former professor at the Van Helsing Academy responsible for teaching Black Magic. At one time, Faustius was a trusted confidante of Lothar Van Helsing, but Faustius was dismissed from his post over a year ago. His current whereabouts are unknown.

FIELD OBSERVATIONS:

- Fluent in multiple languages

- Seen conducting meetings with known operatives of the Dark Ones organization

- Very intelligent

- Anxious and paranoid

STATUS: ACTIVE TARGET

DEPARTMENT OF SUPERNATURAL INVESTIGATIONS

CHAPTER FIFTEEN

COUNT DOWN

My mind is blown.

Faustius just told me I'm the Blood Grail!

What?

At first, I think he's nuts. But the more I think about it, the more it makes perfect sense. After all, I'm supposedly the only living ancestor of Count Dracula. So, if Faustius needs Count Dracula's Supernatural blood to bring him back to life, there's only one place to get it from.

Me!

Suddenly, everything that's happened becomes crystal clear. Now I understand why those werewolves wanted me. Faustius sent them to capture me alive so he could get my blood. When that failed—twice—he manipulated Aura to find his cursed book and teleport me into his lab. I've got to hand it to him, he's persistent.

But that's not all he's been up to.

Faustius was also the one who sent the zombies to rob those graves. And if his master plan comes to fruition, he'll stick Dracula's spirit into their bones and take over the world!

Now, if I wasn't watching Dracula's spirit ping-ponging around the room, I'd say the whole thing was impossible. But this looks like it's about to go down!

Faustius lifts my arm and positions the chalice beneath it. Then, he raises his scalpel.

Holy cow!

He's really going to do it!

He's going to cut me!

I feel like I'm about to pass out, but I can't. I've got to stop him before it's too late!

"Faustius," I plead, "think this through. Is this really a good idea? Let's say your theory is correct and I'm the Blood Grail. If you bring Count Dracula back to life do you really think you can control him? I mean, he's Count. Freaking. Dracula. You know, the King of Darkness. Do you think he's going to listen to you?"

"A valiant attempt," Faustius says. "But I am not worried. I can control Dracula."

"Ha!" I blurt out. "Just like you controlled that demon you needed Van Helsing's help to destroy?"

"Enough!" he says enraged. "You don't know what you're talking about! Without me, Dracula would remain an amorphous spirit. I will control him, and he will do my bidding!"

SLASH!

Ahhh!

My right arm is on fire!

I look down and see a thin cut on the top of my forearm. There's red liquid on Faustius' scalpel.

H-He cut me!

"Finally!" Faustius says, holding up my arm. "The sweet elixir I've been seeking."

I'm horrified. All I can do is watch as my blood drips into the chalice. Then, when he's satisfied he's collected enough, he drops my arm onto the table and walks over to the skeleton.

"Do not worry, Bram," he says. "When I am finished your pain will be over quickly. I will ensure Count Dracula sees to that. After all, only a vampire can truly kill another vampire."

My arm is throbbing, but I'm still strapped in, so I can't stop the bleeding. I'm woozy, but I need to stay conscious. I've got to get out of here before it's too late.

"Prepare, Dracula!" Faustius commands, pouring my blood over the bones of the skeleton. "Prepare to rejoin the land of the living!"

Dracula's spirit is swirling over the skeleton.

"Watch the boy," Faustius orders the werewolves. "I must focus on the task at hand."

Whatever hold Faustius had on me relaxes because I can suddenly move again. But I can't pull out of the arm or leg restraints. I'm losing blood quickly, getting dizzier by the second. There's no way I can use my vampire abilities even if I wanted to.

Faustius begins chanting, his voice growing louder.

Thunder CRACKS outside and the wind picks up, blowing into the room.

Faustius raises his arms. He's concentrating, eyes closed, repeating the same words over and over again.

The next thing I know, the black mist forms a shape. I-Is that a bat? But then it disperses rapidly, flowing over the bones, covering them completely. Then, the skeleton starts smoldering and black smoke billows into the air.

I-It's working!

I have to stop it!

I try sitting up to bust the arm shackles, but the werewolves GROWL and push me back down. My energy is sapped, and my eyelids are getting heavy. I try keeping them open, but I can't.

Everything is blurry.

I'm blacking out.

HOOT!

W-What's that? An owl?

HOOT!

That sounded louder. Strangely familiar.

I force my eyes open, and I can't believe what I'm seeing. It's a girl. Floating down from the ceiling.

I-Is that an angel?

"SCOOT!" she says.

Scoot?

OMG!

Aura!

She's alive! Well, I mean, she's not dead! Well… it's just great to see her!

I feel overwhelmed with emotion.

"Bram!" she yells. "Stop gawking and get moving!"

Aura furrows her brow and my restraints pop open!

But how? Then, I realize Aura used her telekinesis to free me!

"I'll distract these guys," Aura says, lowering herself to the ground. "You stop Faustius. Now catch me if you can you hairy morons!"

Aura takes off with the werewolves in hot pursuit.

She's right. I've got to stop Faustius. But blood is running out of the cut on my arm. First things first. I grab a bandage off the small table and wrap it around my forearm to stop the bleeding. Then, I glance over at Faustius.

He's so focused on what he's doing, he's got no idea what's going on over here. But something weird is happening to the skeleton. It's like it's being wrapped in layers of black energy. It almost looks like the energy is forming into… muscles?

Count Dracula!

Instinctively, I close my eyes and think.

How can I stop Faustius?

An image of a flying bat pops into my mind.

That's it! If I can turn into a bat, I can attack Faustius and stop all of this before it's too late. But can I turn into a bat? I mean, it's never worked before. But then I stop myself. There's no time to dwell on the past. I shake the negative thoughts from my mind and concentrate.

I focus like I've never focused before.

I picture a bat.

I can become a bat. I must become a bat.

I lock in on that image.

Then, I start to believe.

Suddenly, I feel my body... transforming? My limbs begin to recess. My fingers extend, curling into sharp claws. Something sprouts from the underside of my arms. Are those wings?

Then, the world around me changes.

I pick up sounds I've never heard before, like the wind swishing around the skeleton's body. Strange odors assault my nostrils, like the sweat from Faustius' skin. New colors from hidden spectrums strike my eyes with blinding intensity. It's like a sensory overload. What happened?

Then, I realize I'm a bat.

I-I did it!

But there's no time to celebrate.

I start flapping my arms and lift into the air. I beat my wings furiously, totally unsure of how to do this flying thing when my head SMASHES into the ceiling.

Ouch! Too much flapping.

I adjust my flutter rate, and then divebomb Faustius, digging my toes into his back.

"Ahhh!" Faustius screams, breaking his chant.

I flap my wings in his face, pummeling him as best I can, but he's inherently stronger and pushes me away.

"Is that you, Bram?" he says. "I don't know how you got free, but I'm impressed. Unfortunately, you are too late. The deed is done."

I want to respond, but I'm a bat. I manage a "SHRIEK!" and dive in for round two.

I get in a few more shots before Faustius grabs one of my wings and SLAMS me to the ground.

Ugh. My whole left side hurts.

I try righting myself, but I'm seeing stars. That really knocked me for a loop. Then, the area around me darkens. It's Faustius. And this time he's holding a large knife!

I try to fly away, but I'm in too much pain.

"I think it's time you were grounded," Faustius says. "For good."

He reaches up to deliver the final blow when a silver arrow suddenly penetrates his arm.

"Augh!" Faustius screams, the knife clanging to the floor.

What the—? What's going on?

"Step away from the boy," comes a familiar voice.

I turn to see Van Helsing standing in the doorway, a silver crossbow in his arms. Then, he fires two more arrows at lightning speed, and I hear werewolves YELPING in the distance.

Despite his gruesome injury, Faustius shouts out a

strange incantation, and the next thing I know, Van Helsing's crossbow leaps out of his hands and flies across the room, smashing into a wall.

I know I'm a sitting bat just lying here, so I focus my energy on turning back to kid-form. It's a struggle, but I concentrate hard. Just then, I feel my limbs expanding, my wings retracting, my body growing bigger.

And then, I'm back.

But I'm so weak.

"Bram, are you okay?" Aura asks, appearing next to me from out of nowhere.

"Not sure yet," I say, breathing heavily.

"How?" Faustius cries, backing up to the wall, his wounded arm hanging limply at his side. "How did you find me? I-I set a trap for you."

"Yes, you did," Van Helsing says. "But details were never a strength of yours. Let's just say your organization now has several dozen openings to fill. As to how I found this place, I used this." Van Helsing turns his wrist.

It's a Spirit Sensor!

"Professor Morris lent it to me before our so-called appointment," Van Helsing says. "Coincidentally, it was already set to track a certain ghost you have on the premises."

Aura looks at me and smiles.

But my joy quickly turns to horror as I look at the metal table. The skeleton... it's gone!

Just then, something huge drops from the ceiling.

"Headmaster!" Aura cries.

A robed figure lands in a crouch, cutting us off from Van Helsing. It's a man—an absolute giant of a man—with broad shoulders, wispy black hair, and a chalky white complexion. He's wheezing, and I can see his ribs expanding and contracting through his paper-thin skin—like he hasn't breathed for thousands of years. Then, he lifts his head, revealing wild, red eyes.

I-It's… Count Dracula!

"Heaven help us," Van Helsing mutters. "Faustius, what have you done?"

"Isn't it obvious?" Faustius says, grinning from ear to ear. "I have done the impossible. I have brought Count Dracula back from the spirit world. Now bow before me, King of Darkness. Bow and show everyone your gratitude towards me, your High Lord, the man who brought you back to the land of the living."

Count Dracula rises unsteadily, and I realize how shockingly tall he is. He hesitates for a moment, regaining his balance, and then steps towards Faustius.

"Yes!" Faustius screams. "Bow before your creator!"

To my amazement, Dracula approaches Faustius and kneels before him. Faustius' expression is one of pure glee. I-I can't believe it. He's doing it. He's actually controlling Count Dracula!

"M-My Lord," Count Dracula stammers. His voice barely a whisper.

"Yes," Faustius' responds. "Speak, my loyal subject."

Out of the corner of my eye, I catch Van Helsing quietly inching towards his fallen crossbow.

"My Lord," Count Dracula says, "I am forever in your debt for restoring my spirit and providing this magnificent vessel in which I can once again walk this earth. Were it not for you, I would be forced to live out my days as an ethereal being for all of eternity. Now I am free to repay you in any capacity you require. But at the moment, I am quite vulnerable and cannot help but notice there is a descendent of my ancient rival Abraham Van Helsing present. Therefore, I must make one small request before pledging my undying servitude."

"Yes," Faustius says. "Of course. What is it?"

"Sustenance," Count Dracula says. Then, he reaches up and runs a finger down Faustius' wounded arm. When he pulls it away, it's covered in blood.

Faustius recoils, his eyes wide.

"And that sustenance," Count Dracula says, licking Faustius' blood off of his finger, "will be you."

"Faustius!" Van Helsing yells. "Run!"

But Count Dracula grabs Faustius with remarkable speed.

"No!" Faustius screams, and then his eyes roll back in his head. He passed out!

Count Dracula catches Faustius' limp body and throws it over his shoulder. Then, he wheels on me.

Our eyes meet.

I can't look away.

I feel incredibly hot.

Feverish.

"Thank you," he says, revealing long, sharp fangs. "Like Faustius, you have fulfilled your role in the first phase of my plan."

Plan? What's he talking about?

"We shall meet again."

Then, with prey in hand, he jumps and breaks through the glass ceiling in one incredible leap.

Van Helsing grabs his crossbow and fires, but his arrow misses the mark.

They're gone.

And Count Dracula is free to terrorize the world.

"What now?" Aura asks.

"Now?" Van Helsing says solemnly. "Now we prepare for war."

It's all my fault. I feel like a failure.

"I-I'm sorry," I say.

"No, Bram," Aura says. "It's okay. It's not…"

But I never hear the rest of her sentence.

Because I'm out.

EPILOGUE

THE END OF THE BEGINNING

I'm running through the woods at incredible speed.

A full moon hangs in the night sky. There's a chill in the air, but it feels refreshing against my skin.

Everything is a blur as I weave through trees, duck beneath branches, and leap over fallen logs. I'm fast, but I've never run this fast before. The only sounds I hear are my feet crunching on fallen leaves.

As I run, my fists swing in front of me, but they don't look like my fists. They're much bigger than I remember, and they're chalky white.

I want to slow down, but I can't. It's like I'm not in control, like I'm a passenger in someone else's body.

What's going on?

Then, up ahead in the distance, is a building situated in the middle of a swamp. As I slosh through murky, ankle-deep water, it becomes clearer the building is an old manor covered by black vines.

What's it doing here in the middle of nowhere?

Just then, my facial muscles contort into a smile, and

my tongue slides over my teeth, slithering over two very sharp points.

They almost feel like... fangs?

OMG!

***

I spring up in a cold sweat.

What's happening?

Was that a dream?

Or...?

"At last," comes a gentle voice. "You are awake."

I turn to find Van Helsing staring at me. He's sitting in a chair, bundled up as usual, his neck wrapped snugly in a wool scarf. He's leaning forward with his fingers pressed in a steeple position. I notice his silver crossbow propped against the wall.

For a second, I'm totally lost. And then I realize I'm hooked up to several machines, which can only mean one thing. I'm in the infirmary. How did I get here?

Then, it all comes flooding back.

Faustius. The werewolves. Count Dracula...

"Aura!"

"Do not distress," Van Helsing says calmly. "She is fine. Perfectly fine."

I lie back down. Well, at least that's good news. But honestly, Van Helsing is the last person I want to see right now.

"Much has happened," he says. "I am sure you have many questions for me."

He's right about that. I have a million questions, but I don't think I can face him without losing my cool. After all, he lied to me. I wish he'd leave me alone.

"What would you like to know?" he asks. "You can ask me anything."

Too little too late is all I can think. But I figure I'll throw him a bone and maybe he'll leave.

"Is that the Crossbow of Purity?" I ask.

"Yes," he says, raising an eyebrow. "I didn't realize you knew about it."

"Seward covered it," I say. "He asked about it on one of his quizzes."

"Of course," he says. "Is there anything else?"

"Nope," I say. "I'm good. Thanks for stopping by."

"Bram," he starts, "I am—"

"If the next word you're going to say is 'sorry,' then don't bother." I'm fuming mad. I look down at my right forearm which is covered in bandages. That's where Faustius cut me and used my blood to resurrect the evilest villain in the history of the world.

"I am truly sorry," he says with deep sincerity. "I understand why you are angry with me. I am disappointed in myself."

I'm ready to fire back with all the fury I can muster, but I can't. His apology took the wind out of my sails. But I still can't forgive him.

"Well," I say, "I'm still upset."

"I understand," Van Helsing says, his head down.

"I mean, why didn't you tell me I was the Blood Grail? Don't you think that's something I should've known?"

"You are right," Van Helsing says. "I should have told you. It was unfair of me not to. The truth is that I thought it would be too much too soon. I never expected you to be so bold as to break into Faustius' office. Just as I never expected Faustius would lay a trap for you there."

"Right, then there's that creep," I say, feeling agitated all over again. "Faustius told me you're using me. He said only a vampire can kill another vampire. He said you'll sacrifice me to kill Count Dracula."

"I would never do that," Van Helsing says, shaking his head. "I hope you realize Faustius is an opportunist. He would say anything to sway you to his side. But he was not completely wrong."

"What?" I say, sitting up again. "What does that mean?"

"He was correct in saying that only a vampire can truly kill another vampire," Van Helsing says. "Make no mistake, as the last vampire you have a tremendous responsibility. Only you can destroy Count Dracula. But I would never use you. I only intended to train you, so you can come out of this alive."

"Great job you're doing," I mutter.

"I admit, things could be going better," he says, "but

I saw you transform into a bat. That tells me we have accomplished quite a lot. It also tells me your powers are within your control, a very positive development."

"A whole lot of good it did me," I say. "I just helped Count Dracula come back to life."

"You are not to blame," Van Helsing says. "We cannot rewrite the past, we can only shape the future. But yes, it is true, your blood is now running through Count Dracula's body. But you are not at fault. You fell victim to an evil plot far darker than even I could have imagined, yet one I should have seen coming. Do not give up, Bram. Never give up. Count Dracula is out there, growing stronger night by night."

At the sound of his name, I remember my strange dream. It actually felt like I was him. Like I was the one running through the woods in his body. And clearly, he was a lot stronger than when I saw him last. I want to tell Van Helsing about it, but something holds me back.

"What happened to Faustius?" I ask.

"I fear the worst," Van Helsing says. "He always teetered on the fringes of darkness—all the way to the bitter end."

"That's sad," I say.

"Indeed," Van Helsing continues. "But darkness is an unyielding adversary. It entices the weak—just as it enticed Faustius. Left to its own devices, it would doom us all. But together we can fight against it. Together, we can break its evil lure. I cannot force you to help us. I only hope that you will."

Despite my desire to run away, I know I can't.

After all, I'm the one responsible for bringing Count Dracula back to life. Everything that happens from here on out is my fault. I could never walk away knowing that.

So, no matter how dangerous it's going to be, I know I have to fix the problem I created. It's all up to me.

"Don't worry," I say. "I'll stick it out. But you're going to have to tell me everything from now on. And you can't leave anything out. Deal?"

"Deal," Van Helsing says, offering his hand.

We shake just as my friends pile through the door.

I see Rage, Hairball, and Stanphibian. And I'm sure InvisiBill is around here somewhere.

"Glad you're okay," Rage says, greeting me with a high five. "We were worried when we lost track of you in Faustius' office."

"Trust me," I say. "I'm glad to be back."

But someone is missing.

"Where's Aura?" I ask.

"Right here," she says, phasing through the wall.

"Please, not again," Rage says, holding his chest.

Everyone laughs.

Seeing her is a huge relief.

"I'm… happy you're okay," I say.

"I'm glad you're okay too," she says. "And thanks for trying to save me again. You're alright in my book."

"Please," InvisiBill says, "don't say 'book!'"

Everyone laughs.

"Oh, I've got your badge," I say, reaching for my pocket when I realize I'm in a hospital gown. "Well, I'm sure it's around here somewhere."

"Thanks," she says. "But we've got something for you."

For me?

"What is it?" I ask.

"Hairball," Aura says, "hand it over."

"Here ya go," Hairball says. "Catch."

Then, he flips a shiny object into the air. I catch it and turn it over. It's a silver badge!

Engraved in the center is the word:

BRAMPIRE

Brampire?

What's that? Then it hits me.

"No way!" I say. "Really?"

"Really," Rage says. "That's your new code name. Get it, Bram plus vampire equals Brampire. So Brampire, let me be the first to officially welcome you to the Monstrosities."

All the kids clap.

The Monstrosities? I made the team? I don't know what to say. I've never belonged to anything before. I feel tears welling up in my eyes.

"Congratulations, Brampire," Aura says with a wink.

"Thanks," I manage.

"Hey, don't get all sappy," Rage says, patting me on the shoulder. "You don't want Hexum seeing you like this."

He's right about that.

Then, I feel a hand squeeze my shoulder.

"Congratulations," Van Helsing says, leaning in. "Brampire. It has a nice ring to it."

As my friends start busting on each other, I lie back, holding my badge to my chest, happy to be part of the team.

And for the moment, I even forget about my looming destiny—my showdown with Count Dracula.

GET MONSTER PROBLEMS 2 TODAY!

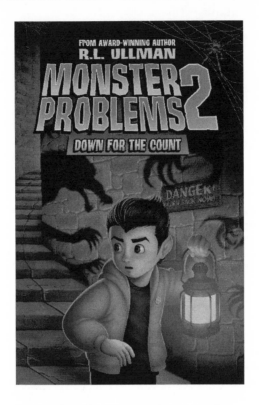

When the school's protection against evil is compromised, everyone is in danger. That's because hidden in the academy is an artifact capable of plunging the world into darkness. If Dracula finds it, he'll conquer the world unhindered by daylight. Bram must stop him, but did he put the school in danger in the first place?

Read Monster Problems 2 Today!

DON'T MISS EPIC ZERO!

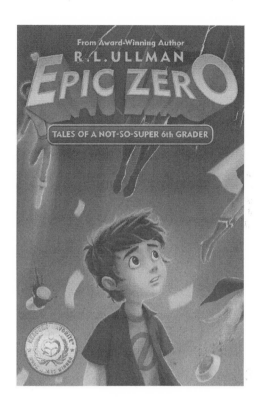

Growing up in a superhero family is cool, unless you're powerless...

Gold Medal Winner - Readers' Favorite Book Awards

Epic Zero: Tales of a Not-So-Super 6th Grader is the first book in a hilarious, action-packed series that will entertain kids, middle school students, and adults!

YOU CAN MAKE A BIG DIFFERENCE

Calling all monsters! I need your help to get Monster Problems in front of more readers.

Reviews are extremely helpful in getting attention for my books. I wish I had the marketing muscle of the major publishers, but instead, I have something far more valuable, loyal readers, just like you! Your generosity in providing an honest review will help bring this book to the attention of more readers.

So, if you've enjoyed this book, I would be very grateful if you could leave a quick review on the book's Amazon page.

Thanks for your support!

R.L. Ullman

ABOUT THE AUTHOR

R.L. Ullman is the bestselling author of the award-winning EPIC ZERO series and the award-winning MONSTER PROBLEMS series. He creates fun, engaging page-turners that captivate the imaginations of kids and adults alike. His original, relatable characters face adventure and adversity that bring out their inner strengths. He's frequently distracted thinking up new stories, and once got lost in his own neighborhood. You can learn more about what R.L. is up to at rlullman.com, and if you see him wandering around your street please point him in the right direction home.

For news, updates, and free stuff, please sign up for the Epic Newsflash at rlullman.com.

***

As always, I would like to thank my Supernatural wife, Lynn, and my freakishly creative kids, Matthew and Olivia, for their undying support.

Made in the USA
Monee, IL
22 November 2020